M000206050

WARNING

This book contains sexually explicit scenes and adult language. It may be considered offensive to some readers. This book is for sale to adults ONLY.

* * * * * * * * * * * * * * * * * *

Please store your files wisely where they cannot be accessed by underage readers.

Other books by Shyla Starr:

Elusive Billionaire Romance Series

Billionaire Hendrick is trying to repair his company's image by putting in some volunteer work, building a school and hospital for the impoverished children in Africa. There, he meets a beautiful African American volunteer, Jocelyn. They hit it off right away but does she belong in his world?

Lonely Billionaire Romance Series

Tricia was hired to care for billionaire John's wife, who is dying. An unlikely romance emerges after his wife, Rebecca, gives John permission to pursue his happiness after she is gone.

Ardent Billionaire Romance Series

Deirdre doesn't know what to make of the gorgeous man that seems to be interested in her. His name is Parker Walters and he seems friendly enough. There is just something off about him. Why is he trying the hide the fact that he is the heir to his father's billion dollar software empire?

Fervent Billionaire BWWM Romance Series

Alexandra had never been with a white man before. She had seen William at the café before but she always kept her distance. It was unfortunate that their first chance meeting happened when she dropped her breakfast and spilled coffee all over his expensive business suit.

Audacious Billionaire BWWM Romance Series

Chante is torn between staying close to a man beyond her league, and fleeing from him to spare herself from a hopeless position. But she finds she is propelled into a place where she needs to confront her doubts and cast her fate aside to follow the dictates of her heart. Damned if she does and miserable is she doesn't, how will Chante face the events that will lead her to a place of pure happiness or to the pits of a broken heart?

Get the latest update on new releases from the author at:

http://shylastarr.com/newsletter

This book is Part One of the "Tenacious Billionaire BWWM Romance Series"

1 - Love Deceived

Adalia is too proud to accept help from the billionaire playboy, Trent Dawson. How long can she maintain her resolve? The bank is at her heels to repossess her business. To make matters worse, Adalia finds suspicious evidence of Trent's philandering ways. She must determine whether to trust Trent with the fate of her business and her heart.

2 - Love Forgiven

Adalia is broken after a keen betrayal and the loss of her lifelong dream: her very own bakery. But she has to carry on, especially now that she's back living under her father's roof and has her semi-abusive ex-boyfriend's advances to contend with. She's determined to continue baking, even if she has to work at the local market for the rest of her days, but she can't shake thoughts of Trent and what happened between them.

3 - Love Endured

Adalia Montclair is determined to be more than Mrs. Dawson. She's going to start her own catering business. But a surprise pregnancy throws a wrench in the works, in the form of her new husband himself. Trent is determined to keep Adalia safe, even if it means keeping her at home and away from her dreams, a fate she can't abide, even with a baby on board. Still, even with tension growing, Adalia can't keep her eyes or hands off her husband.

4 - Love Everlasting

Adalia has just received the worst news of her entire life. Her son, Isaac, is gravely ill, and the only way to save him is a revolutionary treatment which will cost a lot of money. But a lot of money is exactly what Trent doesn't have, now that Space Inc. has gone under. Time is running out and only by working together can Adalia and Trent save their son. Their son's illness and Michelle's interference threatens to tear them apart, but Adalia isn't one to give up that easily.

Tenacious Billionaire BWWM Romance Series

Love Deceived

Book One

By Shyla Starr

© Revelry Publishing 2016

Table of Contents

Chapter One

"**I LIKE** your buns." The customer's voice was creamy, with a hint of spice. "How much are they?"

"Excuse me?" Adalia glanced up from behind the cash register and glared at the man.

"Your buns," he answered, flashing a naughty grin at her.

Heat erupted in her core.

It was him. The guy. He came in every day in that Prada suit, no suitcase, and flaunted his perfect jawline and wavy blond hair. Adalia's stomach did a turn, but she steadied herself mentally.

Come on, it's just a customer. Same as any other in the bakery.

"Can I help you with something?" She asked the same question each day when he came in. Then it would begin.

"That depends." The gorgeous man strolled over and rested his elbows on the glass of the counter that displayed treats and sweets.

"On what, exactly? It's pretty simple," she answered. "Either you want the buns or you don't."

"Oh," he replied, interlocking his fingers and resting his chin on them. "I want the buns. You can count on that." He reached out and brushed her forearm with the tips of his fingers. Sparks danced across her ebony skin.

Adalia cleared her throat gently, but didn't move away. It was the first time he'd touched her, and she'd honestly fantasized about the moment for weeks.

"Which buns would you like?" She breathed the words, and he leaned in close enough that she caught a whiff of his cologne. It was a masculine, woody scent and it suited him perfectly.

Warning alarms went off in her head – this guy was clearly a player, well put together, with that easy charm – but they were drowned out by her attraction to him.

"Yours," he uttered, "every day, for the next month. Every night, too."

Adalia narrowed her chocolate brown eyes at him. She'd given up trusting anyone a long time ago, let alone suave white strangers with a clear desire for more than a carb fix.

"I wouldn't advise you eat that many carbs. And you've yet to specify which type of buns you'd like, sir." She gave a sweet smile she didn't feel in her gut.

Why couldn't she shake her attraction to this guy? She'd just gotten out of a relationship with DeShawn, just started the healing process. She had to focus on getting the bakery on track, not on some sexy dude with a fetish for curvy women.

God, wouldn't it be nice if he had a fetish for – No!

He studied her expression with a grin that made her insides go melty like tempered chocolate.

"I think you know which buns I want."

"Cinnamon," she answered, reaching over for a brown paper bag beneath the glass fronted cabinet. In the back, one of her bakers slammed a tray in the oven and cursed.

Irritation flickered through her – they never treated those ovens with respect – but she kept a straight face.

"No, no," he answered, then grasped her wrist again, and heat waves assaulted her. "I'm in the mood for chocolate today."

She stared him dead in the eye, willing the arousal to back the hell down. "Smooth," she said wryly.

"Excuse me, miss. I'd like to pay?" said a hunched over granny, clasping a box of éclairs.

"Sorry, ma'am," Adalia replied, sparing a frown for the handsome businessman. He winked a blue eye at her and she swallowed hard. "That will be five dollars."

"Five dollars," the lady answered, squinting a little and stretching to pat her curlers. Adalia glanced at 'Handsome Guy' again. He hadn't looked away, and their gazes were glued for a moment. "I'll tell you, it's a pity these éclairs are so good, dearie. You're going to have me on the streets at this rate."

"I'm glad you like them," Adalia replied. That was the plain truth: with the bills piling up, every happy customer helped pave the pathway to financial success. Losing her lifelong dream wasn't an option. "Can I get you anything else?"

"Oh no, dear. Perhaps the recipe so I can make these for myself at home." The old woman's wrinkled façade split into a friendly smile. "No, I'm joking, of course. I quite enjoy the trip into the city for these treasures." She lifted one from the bag and took a bite. Cream squished out the sides and smeared onto her cheek.

"I'll get you a napkin." Adalia fumbled for them beside the register, but Handsome Guy was already on it.

He swept out a handkerchief and handed it to the customer with a courteous bob of his head.

"Thank you," the lady breathed, accepting it with a flutter of her eyelids. "My, what a dashing young fellow. You certainly are a lucky woman." She directed that at Adalia.

"What? He's not my –"

"Not as lucky as I am," he put in, and gestured for the customer to keep the soft square of linen. She thanked him and shuffled out with a cheery wave, pink slippers slapping on the linoleum.

Adalia had given the bakery a fifties' style look. She'd loved the idea of a parlor where customers could sit and have a milkshake while they ate their baked goods. So far, the idea hadn't taken off.

The booths and chairs were empty. A pang of regret stabbed at her stomach, and she wiped down her flowered apron with a grimace.

"I'll get those chocolate buns for you," she said to the businessman, but the stare he gave her made her stop dead in her tracks. "What is it? You don't want them anymore?"

"I do, but I'd prefer it if you had a few with me. Do you make coffee here?"

"We do," she said, "but I've got way too much to do to take a break."

"I wasn't asking."

"Look, I don't even know your name. What makes you think you can come in here, flirt with me and make a fool out of me in front of my customers?" Adalia allowed anger to gutter through her and override the desperate need to reach out and spank that cute butt. "Now, if you want buns, I'll give you buns, but I'm going to have to ask you to leave."

"I assume you don't normally treat your customers this way." He glanced left and right, searching the empty storefront with mock intrigue.

"How I treat my customers is none of your business," she snapped. He'd hit a nerve there. The bakery was her life, her dream and her future, and it was falling through her fingers so fast, she barely had time to jam them shut.

Sunlight filtered through the front window, highlighting the golden streaks in his hair.

Adalia turned her back on him and got the damn chocolate buns, then thrust them at him over the counter. He took out a leather wallet with a flourish and flipped it open, but she shook her finger at him.

"No," she said, "these are free of charge."

"That's nice of you," he said, his left eyebrow lifted, and she longed to smack him in it. Then kiss him. Kiss him all over.

"It's free of charge because I don't consider you a customer. Don't come back here again. Understand?" She folded her arms and steadied her breathing.

The devilishly attractive businessman ran his thumb down his jaw, holding the brown bag aloft. "Sorry," he said, without a smidgen of the remorse he professed, "but I'm not in the habit of making promises I can't keep."

"Get out," she hissed at him.

He strolled to the door with a low chuckle and pulled it open with a tinkle of the bell. "I'll see you tomorrow, Adalia."

"How did you know my –?"

But he didn't let her finish, cutting across her with one word. It cut her to ribbons, zigzagged through the air between them on vibrations of smoldering need.

"Trent."

Then he was gone.

Chapter Two

Adalia slammed the door of the fridge so hard, a few of the cute kitty magnets fell off and scattered across the tiles.

"Damn," she whispered, then placed the bottle of wine on the kitchen counter and bent to collect the kittens. She rearranged them haphazardly and grimaced at the bill she'd stuck up on the beige surface of the refrigerator.

The bakery wasn't in the clear, and the bank wanted the money back. Now. There were too few customers, or too many expenses, and it ate at her that she couldn't make it work.

"No. I will make this work. I will." She grabbed the wine bottle, popped the cork and sloshed some of the deep red fluid into a glass. Failure wasn't an option... it wasn't in her vocabulary.

She'd grown up too poor and worked too hard to let that happen.

Adalia strolled through to her living room and lowered herself to the couch with a sigh. She'd not bothered to take off her apron, and she'd been home a half hour. There was just too much to do.

Her laptop was laid out on her wooden coffee table, open and glaring at her, coaxing her to swap over from the spreadsheet to an episode of *Game of Thrones*.

There wasn't a TV in the apartment, but she preferred it that way. Anything she really wanted to watch was on Netflix and she was too busy for shows most nights anyway, but after the weird encounter with the mysterious Trent, all she wanted was a glass of wine, some leftover pizza and a couple of dragons.

An email notification sounded on the laptop, and she leaned forward with a frown.

It was from a woman named Michelle Van Heerden.

Attn: Adalia,

We would like to hire you to cater an event. Please respond with contact details so we may discuss this over the phone.

Regards,

Ms. Van Heerden

Adalia took a sip of wine and rattled off a quick response with her phone number. This was good news – she couldn't help allowing the hope to burgeon in her chest.

Riiiing.

She jumped and swept up her cell, then pressed the green button without checking who the call was from.

"Adalia speaking," she said, injecting confidence into her voice, which was part alcohol inspired and part innate.

"Hey, girl," a deep gravelly voice said, and the hair on the back of her neck stood on end.

Great. Just what she needed on a lonely Monday night: not a potential client, but her lowlife ex-boyfriend.

"DeShawn, I told you not to call me."

"I can't not call you, babe. I miss you too bad." An explosion of raucous laughter drowned out another sentence, but it wasn't a loss to her ears.

"You're high again," Adalia stated, resolved to the answers and the lies he'd tell to get out of the telling the truth.

"No, course not, baby. You told me to stop, so I did, right?" he said it in a mild slur and she rolled her eyes.

"And you've been drinking as well. You need to get that drunk dial app on your phone, DeShawn." She couldn't help cracking jokes, though he probably wouldn't get that he was the butt of it.

"What that?"

"Never mind. I'm going to blacklist your number, so don't try calling again." She pressed the red button with relish and slapped the phone down on the table. How had she ever dated him?

The constant lack of ambition, sitting at home all day and smoking pot while she was out busting her balls for them. Earning as much as she could to fund his boozing and smoking.

It made her livid. Not because he'd wasted his life away or her time for that matter, but because she'd allowed that in her life.

She was a strong woman. Her mother had been a strong woman. Why had she let him walk all over her?

She grabbed at her stomach and frowned. Maybe it was because of self-esteem. Well, she couldn't be anyone other than who she was.

She certainly deserved better than DeShawn.

Adalia took another gulp of wine, then shook her head to clear her thoughts.

Riiiiing.

She gave a low growl and snatched the phone off the coffee table again, shifting the lifestyle and cookery magazines to the right. She set the glass on the table to better handle the call.

DeShawn just didn't know when enough was enough.

"I told you, I'm going to blacklist your damn number, so do not call me back!" Adalia hovered her finger of the red button to hang up.

"Is that Adalia?" a snooty woman asked, and Adalia's heart leapt into her throat. She flashed to the email she received earlier. It was most likely the potential client.

Embarrassment heated her cheeks, and she fanned herself with one hand. "That's correct."

"Is this a bad time, Ms. Montclair?" The woman's cool answer cut at her sense of professionalism.

"Not at all, I've just been receiving continuous calls from telemarketers and I've grown quite fed up. I'm sure you can understand." Adalia was quick on her feet at least.

"Of course," the woman answered without changing her tone. "I emailed you about catering for an event. My name is Michelle Van Heerden."

"Yes, thank you, Ms. Van Heerden. May I ask what you require for the event?" She stood and hurried to the kitchen, her stockings slipping her up a little, then snatched up a pen and paper.

"We've got the menu set for the event, but we're lacking a good idea for dessert."

"That's definitely my forte," Adalia answered, though she frowned. How had this woman found her? She wasn't exactly in the papers, and she seriously doubted that Ms. Van Heerden, in all her snobby glory, would deign to leaf through the yellow pages.

"I have it on good authority that your chocolate éclairs are sublime," Van Heerden droned on, seemingly bored by her own conversation. "So, we'd like you to cater for two hundred guests."

"Two hundred," Adalia answered, scribbling the number down and keeping the stammer of awe out of her voice. That was two éclairs per guest, and four hundred in total. "When's the event?"

Van Heerden cleared her throat. "In three days."

Good God. Adalia gripped the pen until it made a crack of protest. She needed the money, but she'd have to work night and day to make that deadline. That was a lot of choux pastry.

"Can you do it, Ms. Montclair?"

Adalia clicked her tongue softly, considering, need and fear mingling inside. "Absolutely, where's the event being held?"

"The NYIT Auditorium on Broadway. This is a charity event and exceptionally important. We expect prompt delivery and service from you, Ms. Montclair."

"Of course. I'll be there, you can count on it," Adalia answered with total confidence.

The line went dead, and Adalia placed her phone in her bag, which lay open on the kitchen counter. Ms. Van Heerden was upper echelon indeed, if she couldn't spare a minute to say 'thank you' or 'goodbye'.

Adalia breathed slowly, staring at the clock on the wall, ticking away. Three days wasn't enough time, but hell, she'd make it work.

She pulled on her shoes, adjusted that apron and slung her bag over her shoulder, then shot a text message off to her assistant patisserie to meet her at the bakery.

Adalia set her gaze on the bill plastered to her fridge and gave a curt nod. This was her chance to make it work, to pay off some of the debt and get the business going.

She left the bottle of wine on the coffee table.

Chapter Three

"I'm relieved you made it, Ms. Montclair,"
Michelle Van Heerden said, teetering beside Adalia in
five-inch high heels and a form-fitting black cocktail
dress.

She was white, blonde and skinny as all hell. Bit of
a hooked nose, though it didn't take away from her
beauty. What did take away from it, however, was that
constant glare of disdain.

"Me?" Adalia placed a hand on the crisp chef's
whites she'd purchased specifically for this job. "I
wouldn't have missed your event for the world, Ms.
Van Heerden." She clicked her fingers and her assistant
bustled in – also in brand spanking new chef's whites –
carting tray upon tray of ingredients.

All they'd have to do is melt the chocolate and
assemble the éclairs and they'd be ready to send plates
out. Underneath her calm exterior, Adalia was
exhausted to the bone. She'd gotten a maximum two
hours sleep a night, and that was usually in the kitchen
of the bakery.

"The client, my boss, has very specific instructions for this meal," Van Heerden droned on, checking the red lacquer on her claw-like nails. "He wants the entire meal done by eight this evening and not a second later. You may begin serving the éclairs at quarter to eight. After the final dish has been served, you may enter the hall to receive thanks along with the other chefs."

"That's unusual." It slipped out before Adalia could catch it. Usually the chefs or caterers were behind-the-scenes personnel, certainly not granted an appearance at the end of a charity event.

"Yes, Mr. Dawson was clear on this point," Van Heerden said and rolled her eyes, then blinked a few times. It was clear she didn't hold with such sentimentality. "He's sponsored this entire event, a charity for inner city kids, and he wants people inspired to give back and be grateful. Time for work?" The woman pointed in the opposite direction.

Adalia wriggled her nose and strolled to her place beside one of the gas-burning stoves.

"She's nice," Jenny said, standing closer and pointing a thumb in Van Heerden's direction and smirking. "In the way that pubic lice is nice, if you know what I mean." The pastry chef had been with her for a while, but she was too talented, and Adalia was pretty nervous she'd disappear soon.

"Yeah, well money is money." She unclipped the lid of the plastic container they'd brought for the chocolate. "We'll do our job, get our pay and get the hell out of here."

"Maybe you'll pick up some more clients out there, who knows?" Jenny patted her on the arm and helped her take out slab upon slab of the chocolate. She was positive about the future of the bakery, but then she didn't know just how much financial trouble it was in.

"Yeah, maybe," Adalia said with a noncommittal shrug.

"Fancy meeting you here," a voice said behind them and they both flinched and turned.

Adalia's insides turned to mulch.

It was Trent.

Jenny gave a tiny gasp then colored bright red from the top of her forehead to the bit of skin poking out at the neck. She coughed, then mumbled something about chocolate and swept up a few slabs. The pastry chef hightailed it out of there without a second glance.

Adalia didn't allow herself to be intimidated. Trent was in Prada this time – she had a keen sense for fashion, it was another calling – and he had that sweltering gaze in place.

"I don't know who allowed you back here, but now is not the time for messing around." Adalia leaned one palm on the counter and gave a long-suffering sigh.

"I never mess around, Adalia. You should know that by now." He stayed where he was, leaving the tension between them rather than closing the distance. She longed to be closer, but she couldn't allow that thought to consume her.

He was hot, that was all. It wasn't as if they had any real connection, other than his love of teasing her.

She gathered up ingredients and went to join Jenny by the stove. "We're going to need a bigger pot for this group. If we split it into three to five batches, we should be able to –"

"I'm not done talking to you." Trent appeared beside them, and Jenny flinched again, then pushed her glasses up her nose.

"Yeah, but I am done talking to you and I have work to do." Adalia studied him with a tiny frown of disapproval. "Something you clearly don't know much about," she muttered and it was as if she'd injected iron into his spine.

Every inch of his body turned stiff, and he stared at her with the strangest expression, a mix of anger and something deeper. Was it need?

No, it couldn't be.

"You'd better run along before the guy in charge kicks you out. What are you doing here anyway?" She was too curious to let the question go unanswered.

Ms. Van Heerden burst into the kitchen, swaying that perfectly groomed head from side-to-side, searching.

Adalia steeled herself for a scolding – under any other circumstance, she wouldn't take it, but this woman was a client.

"Mr. Dawson!"

Trent kept Adalia's gaze, ignoring Michelle in the background. Van Heerden fixed her gaze on his back and bustled over to them.

"Mr. Dawson, they're waiting for you out there." She tapped him on the shoulder, but he didn't turn to her.

"You're Mr. Dawson," Adalia said, her tone peppered with disbelief.

"I'm afraid so," he answered, tucking his hands into his pockets and flexing beneath his suit. His muscles strained at the arms, but it wasn't obscene. The suit accentuated him, resting lightly, tightening in the right places.

Michelle, for her part, was equally well-outfitted, especially with a slender waist to match the open back of that black dress.

And Adalia… she brushed off her chef's whites and restrained a groan of mortification. Her mystery employer was none other than the man she'd been crushing on for a month.

"I see you've met our caterer. One of them, anyway," Van Heerden said, then glanced over toward Adalia, searching for the others she'd hired. "The meal will be ready to start soon, and they're calling for a speech out there, Mr. Dawson."

"Do you have eyes, Michelle?" Trent finally broke his connection with Adalia and turned to his assistant. She pushed her chest outward and pouted slightly. Jealousy crept through Adalia's mind, poking at her sense of calm.

"Sir?"

"Do you have eyes?"

Michelle fluttered her eyelids. "Why, of course, sir."

"So you can see I'm in the middle of a conversation. That's obvious to you?" Trent took his hands out of his pockets and checked his cufflinks.

Michelle's face fell. "Yes, I can see that, sir."

"Then kindly explain to me why you interrupted."

Embarrassment followed close on the heels of the jealousy. Didn't he realize that this was more uncomfortable for her than for them?

"I have to get back to work," Adalia inserted, then made to walk off, but he caught her by the arm and immobilized her with those sparks of desire.

"Not so fast. I believe my assistant owes you an apology, first." Trent gestured toward Michelle and Adalia met her gaze, hating every minute of the entire encounter.

Van Heerden focused on her, but there was no remorse in her, only a bone deep sense of hatred. "Sorry."

Adalia gave a curt nod and broke the contact with both of them. She strode back to the stove – careful not to hurry – and took her place beside Jenny.

"What on earth was that about?" asked Jenny.

Adalia glanced back at Trent, but he'd already left for the main hall.

"I have no idea," she said, stirring the melting chocolate.

Chapter Four

"And none of this would be possible without the stellar chefs and caterers who provided the meal for you this evening," Trent said, standing in front of the crowd of two hundred people, still finishing off the remains of the chocolate éclairs.

Adalia stood with her arms at her sides, back straight and staring straight ahead. If she played this right, she might get more clients. If she didn't, she'd likely lose the bakery.

Either way, it was pretty darn difficult to concentrate with Trent a few feet from her. That cologne was in the air, enticing her with the promise of dreams that night.

"I believe that children should have access to three basic needs," Trent went on, confidence oozing from his every pore. He held up one finger and continued, "The need for food."

Audience members nodded as if this was a breaking news special.

Trent's middle finger came up to join his index. "The need for shelter."

More nods of approval and low murmurs.

The ring finger appeared alongside the other two, and Adalia pressed her lips together, intrigued in spite of her skepticism. "The need for education."

"With these three basic needs met, a child, no matter what his or her upbringing or background, has a fighting chance to succeed in life." He turned to the side and pointed to a screen on the wall behind them. "Which is why we've decided to use your funds to build the Inner City Eat, Live and Learn Shelter for all kids, eighteen and under."

An image of the proposed shelter appeared, and Adalia restrained a gasp. Trent Dawson had a lot of time, money or power – maybe all three – if he could help fund something like this.

It was brick-faced, but with grand entrances, a pool, sports center, basketball courts, dance studio and classrooms.

Trent continued his speech, picking up a laser pointer to indicate the facilities. "Here, the children will have room to board, a safe house if they have no other home or things at their homes aren't what they should be."

He moved the beam along the image and pointed toward the section of classrooms. "They'll be tutored in various topics, including science, math, technology and literature. Everything a private school would offer."

Trent paused and glanced toward Adalia, then moved the laser back to the center of the building. "And here, the children will learn how to cook and bake, giving them the opportunity to follow a culinary career path should they see fit."

Her heart melted in her chest, and her knees shook a little, but she kept herself upright. This kind of thing brought tears to her eyes. She'd been one of those kids. Luckily, she'd had a father who'd worked every day to keep her in school. He'd taught her the lessons of hard work, hard knocks and following your dreams.

"Thanks to your generous donations, we can now make this dream a reality and give hope to children across the city." Trent Dawson finished without bells or whistles. He simply switched the pointer off and placed it on the podium beside him. It didn't roll off onto the plush red carpet.

The audience applauded, rising to their feet, and Trent nodded and waved, but didn't make a big show of himself. He simply gestured to the band, which struck up a chord and the music began.

There was a shrill squeal of delight in the crowd, followed by several gasps. Lana Del Ray, the famous singer, was on the stage, swaying from side-to-side. She sang Ultraviolence, and Adalia's eyes widened. It was one of her favorites.

"Thank you for coming today," Trent said, closing in on her with the future in his gaze. He had her attention now, and he could see it. She couldn't help be taken in by his goals, his choice in music and that heady scent.

It made her feel weak, and she was anything but that.

"Thank you for inviting me." There was no other reply to this.

"Hopefully this brings in a couple customers to that bakery of yours."

"Is that why? I thought it was because you wanted to show off your inner city dream." Adalia couldn't help the hostility. She needed him to know she wasn't easy, she wasn't some blonde assistant bimbo who'd cave to his every need.

I love you the first time

I love you the last time

Yo soy la princesa, comprenda mis white lines

Cos I'm your jazz singer

And you're my cult leader

Lana Del Rey's dulcet tones filled the blanks in their conversation, giving meaning to what Adalia felt. Or what she thought she felt. How was it possible to be this attracted to a man from another world, from another time, from a place she couldn't follow? Not because she wasn't good enough, but because he wouldn't want her to.

She was not a follower.

Trent moved toward her and held out a hand. "Dance with me."

"What's the magic word?" Adalia folded her arms.

"I wasn't asking."

"That's your catchphrase."

He grabbed her and pulled her in close to whisper in her ear. "Have I caught you?"

"Mr. Dawson," Michelle Van Heerden called over the heads of the crowd. They swayed and danced in time to the music, and the song changed. "Trent," she said again, but he didn't pull away from Adalia.

Instead, he lowered his lips to her neck and breathed on her skin, tracing a line from her collar bone up to her ear. "Have I caught you?"

Adalia had disappeared, replaced by a woman she barely knew, one who wanted nothing more than to feel Trent's embrace, his hands on her body. Michelle was near now, clacking across the floor in her stilettos until she reached the carpeted area they stood on.

"Have I caught you?" he asked a third time.

"No," Adalia replied, every nerve screamed at her, begging for his touch. "You can't catch the wind." She detached from him, breaking the connection she'd believed impossible.

She didn't know anything more than his name, and the fact that he was arrogant, but it was as if she'd been with him before. Known his touch, seen forever in those bright blue eyes.

"Trent," Michelle sighed, sidling up to them with assurance. "Everyone is dying to talk to you about the project. They're overwhelmed by the thought of it."

"Overwhelmed is hardly the correct term," he replied, irritation snipping the words off.

Adalia backed off slowly. She didn't need another embarrassing encounter with the chic Ms. Van Heerden and her boss.

Michelle nodded. "I suppose you're right." Then she slipped her arm through his and gripped his bicep. "Though, I must say the entire event went off without a hitch." She prattled on and Trent didn't pay attention to her.

"It's thanks to the chefs and caterers, like Adalia," he replied, smiling.

"Oh, yes, of course. But the planning, the time and effort you put in? That's priceless. It was an honor working with you on this one. Congratulations, sir," she murmured, shooting a triumphant glance at Adalia. She craned her neck upward and kissed him on the cheek, near that flawless jawline covered in stubble.

That jealousy from earlier came back, amplified tenfold. This was bad. This was too much to handle after DeShawn. She'd been right about Trent. He was obviously a player and involved with Van Heerden.

Trent frowned and moved away from Michelle, but it was too late.

"Adalia, come back here." It was a blatant command, and she blatantly ignored it. Adalia Montclair was not a pushover. She tucked the anger and hurt into her core.

"Thank you for the opportunity, Mr. Dawson." Adalia called back as she gave a formal nod, then turned and strolled back to the kitchens.

Chapter Five

"I'm sorry," Jenny whispered.

"I understand. I saw it coming a mile off. It's not your fault, I know you deserve way better than this." Adalia gave a weak smile.

Jenny burst into tears and wiped them away with the back of her hand. Adalia reached into her desk drawer and brought out a box of tissues. She offered them to her pastry chef – ex-pastry chef, now – and Jenny swept one up and used it to blow her nose.

"We built this place together." Jenny sniffled and dabbed at her eyes, shaking her head. "I can't believe I'm not going to work here anymore… it feels like I'm leaving home."

Adalia gave a heavy sigh, and rose from her chair. She circled the small desk and flung her arms around Jenny. "Everybody leaves home at some point. I guess it's fitting that you set yourself free. You'll fly high, Jenny. You're one of the best pastry chefs in the city. It sucks to lose you because of this, but I know there's nothing I can do."

"I could stay," Jenny said, stiffening because of her stubborn streak, going back on the words she'd just spoken.

"I can't afford to pay you what you deserve," Adalia answered. "Hell, I can't even afford to pay you what a dishwasher deserves. It's a shitty situation, and I can't make it better this way."

Jenny sobbed, and Adalia patted her on the back then let go.

"But you can bet I'll be banging down your door the minute I can afford to have you onboard again," she said with a smile. Like that would ever happen. She hadn't seen an increase in customers or requests since the charity event at all. The money had just about run out.

"I'll be waiting for that call." Jenny reached out and grasped Adalia's hands in hers. "Thank you for making me feel like part of your family."

"Oh honey, you are a part of the family." Adalia welled up, the emotion finally breaking her tough exterior. She wanted to ignore the pain and move past it, but she couldn't. Losing Jenny was like losing a sister, and it was proof that her lifelong dream was falling away before her very eyes.

"I'd better get going. Mark is finally moving to the big city!" That was Jenny's fiancée. He'd been in Chicago for a year, making extra cash on the side so he'd be able to afford the wedding.

"That's wonderful. I'm so happy for you," Adalia said, but she was tormented inside. It was a feeling she despised: knowing that she desperately craved love and affection she'd never get.

"It will happen," Jenny whispered, then pecked her on the cheek and disappeared out of the office and probably out of Adalia's life for good.

She went back to her chair and plopped into it, groaning when she hit the hardwood back with force. She couldn't even afford proper office furniture. Too many expenses, too little time to make the money to pay them off.

Adalia pulled out the newest letter from the bank and looked it over. She still owed twenty-thousand dollars on the loan, and they'd grown impatient with her dawdling. She could hardly break even, let alone pay off a debt of that size.

Riiiiing.

Her heart leapt into her throat, but she calmed herself immediately. No way would that be Trent – why had he even popped into her mind? It was ridiculous.

"Hello?"

"Is this Adalia Montclair speaking?" a man wheezed into the phone, and she frowned. It definitely wasn't Trent. Or DeShawn for that matter, thank God.

"Yes, this is she." She pushed the letter to the side and took out a pen and piece of paper. This guy sounded important, and she crossed her fingers. Hopefully he was an audience member from the charity event a week or so ago.

"Ms. Montclair, I'm calling from the bank about your loan repayments."

It was the bank calling in the debt. Not a new client, not a hopeful encounter to help her speed the process of achieving her dream.

"And to whom am I speaking?" Adalia switched to formal mode, and shut down on her fear and all other emotion. When these guys smelled blood in the water, they laid in with twenty sets of teeth. Shark wasn't the word. What was that creature from *Pirates of the Caribbean*?

The Kraken.

They were a bunch of damn Krakens.

"You are speaking with Mr. Samuels from the bank, ma'am."

"Thank you," she said and scribbled the name down. "What can I help you with?" As if she didn't know already.

"We'd like to talk to you about your loan repayments in person, but you've missed your last two meetings."

"Meetings? I haven't received any correspondence about meetings with you people." It was the absolute truth.

"Regardless, the bank has tried to contact you on multiple occasions to set up a viable repayment plan, but you seem to have avoided each attempt. It is now the bank's intention to liquidate your assets, should you be unable to pay the amount in full, by June 15th."

"That's a month from now!" Adalia screeched. Outrage and shock mingled in equal parts and spread through the cells of her body.

"That's the final date for payment. After that, the bank will repossess your assets in order to repay your debt." The man coughed and yawned, and Adalia clenched the pen hard. It snapped clean in half, splattering ink across the paper and the desk.

"How do you expect me to come up with twenty grand in a month?" Adalia asked through gritted teeth, but Mr. Samuels seemed entirely unconcerned by her distress.

"That is entirely up to you, Ms. Montclair."

"Now, you listen –"

Bang!

The office door swung open and DeShawn strolled in, scratching under the line of his do-rag.

"Hey, girl," he said, grinning. He folded his arms and studied her, muscles bulging beneath the wife beater.

"Get out," she shouted then lowered her voice. "Mr. Samuels, you can't be serious about this. I need more time than a month. Please, have some sympathy."

But the staid, old banker had already hung up and the dial tone rang in Adalia's ear. She dropped the phone to the desk and let out a low growl of anger.

"What the hell are you doing here?" She pushed up from the desk and glared at her ex-boyfriend.

"You won't answer my calls. I had to find out if you was okay."

"I'm fine, and I don't need your concern, DeShawn." She motioned for him to leave, but he swaggered around to her side of the desk and grabbed her around the waist.

He pulled her into him, and she slapped him hard across the cheek.

"Don't you dare touch me," she said.

He dropped his arms, the corners of his lips pulled taut. "What we got is special. You can't deny that."

"What we have? We have nothing. All we have are broken bongs and shattered memories. You understand me?" Adalia slapped him again, across the other cheek this time just to even things out.

She was too angry to care she'd hurt him, too upset over losing the bakery. Her dream was as good as gone, and there was no one to blame but herself.

"Why you hitting me? You know better than that." He grabbed her by the face and squished her cheeks.

Adalia's heart was overcome with sorrow. She'd given DeShawn everything, loved him though he'd returned nothing but empty hopes and bullshit. And now he dared harm her? He dared lay hands on her?

She lifted her knee and rammed it into his crotch. He doubled over with a cry of pain and she burst into tears, picked up her bag and walked out of the office.

The bill lay on the desk, staring at the ceiling, the zeroes were like eyes of greed.

Chapter Six

Adalia kneaded the dough, taking out the frustration of the day on the emulsion of flour, water, salt and yeast.

Between the bank and DeShawn's interference, there wasn't much room for calm. Her mind swirled with questions about her future. If she lost the bakery, she'd have nowhere to live. She'd be forced back to her father's place, because there was no way in hell she'd get drawn into DeShawn's web of laziness and lies again.

She paused and wiped her brow with her forearm, then sighed.

There had to be some way for her to make this money back.

The bell over the door in the shop tinkled.

"We're closed!" she called out, frowning to herself. That'd better not be DeShawn. Besides, it was past five already and she'd hung the 'CLOSED' sign in the shop window.

"Hello?" Adalia called, brushing the flour from her hands and onto her apron. "Who's there?"

A trickle of fear worked its way into her mind – this was New York, after all – but she diverted it with thoughts of calm.

She covered the dough with a damp cloth, then tiptoed over to the sink and picked up a chopping knife from beside the sink. She gripped it tight, and the cool steel against her palm gave her shivers.

Adalia waited. Footsteps approached, heavier than a woman's. It definitely was a man, but he didn't have DeShawn's loping gait; that she could recognize within seconds.

"You'd better have a good reason for coming here," she said out loud, using her hardest tone possible, but it still quavered in the middle.

"I always have a reason for everything I do," Trent said, strolling in with that easy confidence he wore around his shoulders like a cape. Did that mean he was a superhero?

She restrained a grimace at the cheesiest thought she'd ever had.

"What are you doing back here?" She laid the knife back on the counter and folded her arms. "This area is off limits to customers."

"I'm not just a customer," he said, walking over to meet her. She didn't move away from him, she couldn't bring herself to back off. There was too much tension between them, too much need.

Still, he had that bimbo, that blonde Van Heerden with her perfect body.

"I've been thinking about you," he said, and reached up to brush her cheek with the tips of his fingers. "Constantly. You live in my brain, Adalia."

"What do you want?" she whispered, not daring to meet his gaze. She focused on the silver clock on the wall, its hands ticking away. Life flowing in and out, the ebb of her emotion swelling beyond her perception.

There was no control for this. How could she resist him?

"Look at me," he murmured, gruff with desire. "Look into my eyes."

"No." She trembled for him, but she couldn't permit this weakness. Looking into his eyes would be like looking into his soul. It would be over.

He ran those fingers down her cheek and rested them on her chin. He didn't grip it or force her, but the pressure of his intent was enough.

Adalia swayed her head to the side and was met by those ice blue pools of spirit. They brimmed with emotion, the kind women dreamed of, and she drew in a breath.

"Look what you've done to me." Trent didn't break away from the moment, but slid his other hand around her back and brought it up to rest at the nape of her neck, controlling her.

"I don't –"

"You've consumed my every thought, and I barely know you."

It was an echo of her thoughts, and she wanted to collapse from hearing them out loud.

"We owe this to ourselves," he groaned, and layered kisses along her neck and throat. They were hot and

wet, soft as she'd ever felt and hot desire rushed
through her.

"Stop," she moaned, shaking for him, shaking for
more, to have it all, but she couldn't give in to this. He
had someone else; he was a player; he didn't really
want anything more than a conquest and she wasn't
that!

She refused to be that for him.

"Adalia," he mumbled and she turned to jelly. Her
knees buckled, but he caught her in those strong arms
and held her upright, pressed against his broad chest.
Trent kissed the sides of her neck this time, opening his
mouth wider, increasing the pressure and nipping her
skin in places.

"Oh God," she groaned, throwing her head back and
embracing the moment. This one pure moment of
pleasure.

Trent stopped and brought his face toward her, to
take their first real kiss.

"No," she stammered. "Not like this, no." Adalia
placed both palms on his chest and pushed herself
away. He held her fast for a second, but released her
with an expression of regret.

"What's the matter?" Trent's brow wrinkled like a flopped soufflé.

"I won't be another one of your bimbos, Mr. Dawson." She walked away from him, swaying her hips, and stood beside the dough, which would be ruined if she didn't place it in a warmer environment to let it rise.

"You seem to have a lot of knowledge about my personal life that I'm not aware of."

"Oh come on," she said, slapping her thighs to warm her hands. "I'm not stupid, Trent. I know what's really going on here. You're looking for a conquest, a little fun on the side. Why else would you have invited me to that event? It was a blatant attempt to show off."

Trent laughed out loud. "You know me so well already, and you seem to have a rather high opinion of yourself if you think you're my conquest."

She glared at him then hid her shame by uncovering the dough and prodding it. It was ruined, and she scooped it off the table and threw it in the bin without further ado.

He was wrong. She didn't have a high opinion of herself. It was quite the opposite, in fact. She'd been beaten down by herself and by DeShawn's lack of attention during their two-year relationship.

The man had seen her as a plaything, not a woman to be respected, just to be used for his own desires.

"You can't figure it out," he observed, folding those muscled arms beneath his white cotton shirt. It was unbuttoned at the neck, open and hinting at the tanned flesh below.

"Please get out of my kitchen," she responded.

Trent walked to the work bench and planted his fists on it, then leaned right over until he was in her face and there was nowhere else to look.

"Let me get real with you for a minute, girl. I want you. I want you and I plan on having you, but not just in the way you think."

She gulped then blinked several times. The way he'd said it was both arousing and terrifying. What did he actually mean with that? Did he want her for sex? Or did he want to be with her in another way?

He studied her reaction then gave a grunt of approval, which made his Adam's apple bob up and down.

"Yeah, that's right. And guess what, Adalia?" Trent didn't move an inch forward or back, but held that same intensity. The steady stare intoxicated her.

"What?" she replied, trying to inject her usual attitude into the question, but failing miserably. There was no way she'd win this one. Though, she didn't want to at this point.

"I always get what I want."

He turned on his heel and marched out of the kitchen without a glance backward.

Chapter Seven

"So you don't know what to do about it?" Sylvester Montclair cut an imposing figure for a man of his age. Late sixties, with a head of neatly cropped gray hair and the beginnings of a bald spot at his crown, he exuded integrity.

"I don't have that many options at the moment." One kept springing to mind, but it was an option Adalia would never take.

She didn't want handouts, and she certainly wouldn't turn to the billionaire who saw her as a conquest, or whatever else he wanted to call it.

"My girl, you've got to do what's best for your future."

"That's what I'm trying to do, Dad, but I don't know how. I'm lost. The bank wants the money back, I've got no one working for me, and the customers just aren't coming in."

"What about your regulars?" Her father scratched his chin, then handed her a bowl of mashed potatoes.

She dished up for herself and passed him the green beans in return.

"I've got two and that's about it."

Sunday night dinners were their tradition. They connected over deep fried Cajun chicken or roast beef, and ended with apple pie and cream. The cooking part was the best. Adalia would arrive early and help her father prep and cook everything.

The apple pie was definitely her favorite part of the endeavor, but she'd hardly enjoyed making it that afternoon.

There was too much to worry about.

"Adalia, we aren't a family of quitters. Your brother has fallen on hard times before and we supported him through it. Do whatever it is you need to do to make it work."

She nodded thoughtfully and popped a forkful of mashed potatoes and gravy into her mouth. It was delicious and she chewed slowly, considering her options.

"I guess the real problem is –"

There was a knock at the front door, followed by a strange whooping noise.

"What the hell?" Sylvester Montclair rose with a frown. He was the papa bear, protective to a fault, and he'd been there for the kids no matter what.

"Adalia!" DeShawn's voice rang out through the front hall, and her heart sank into her stomach. "Adalia, are you in there? Come on out, babe, we gotta talk about this. I don't want to hear no excuses, this is fo' real."

"You've got to be kidding me." She stood quickly but her father waved for her to stay put.

"I'll handle this, don't you worry." He stretched his neck and strode out of the dining room and into the hall.

Adalia crept after him and stood in the doorway, eavesdropping on the conversation. She peered around the corner, careful not to be seen by her ex-boyfriend.

Sylvester opened the door and placed his hand on the doorjamb, blocking DeShawn's entry with his arm.

DeShawn glared at Sylvester through a haze of pot and reddened eyes.

"What up, old man."

Sylvester clenched his jaw and released. He'd never liked DeShawn, and Adalia sorely regretted not listening to her father's advice sooner. "That's Mr. Montclair to you, boy. What do you want?"

"I'm looking for Adalia. I know she always at your house on a Sunday, man." DeShawn craned his neck and tried to see past her father.

Sylvester clicked his fingers under the stoner's nose. "You deaf as well as drugged, boy? Adalia ain't here. Now, get off my front porch before I call the cops."

"You think you better than me?" DeShawn guffawed. "You just some old dude who can't even make no money."

Sylvester was a plumber. He'd finally set up his own business and made just enough money to support himself. They'd grown up poor but there'd always been food on the table.

"Think long and hard about what you say next, DeShawn," he said, and the warning tone he used when he was seconds from getting serious set off alarms in Adalia's head.

"Man, back outta my way," DeShawn answered, and gripped a handful of the old man's shirt.

Sylvester calmly balled up his fist and punched DeShawn in the center of his chest, causing the unwelcome visitor to stumble back and land on his ass. He glared up, swaying slightly from side-to-side, and choked.

"Get out of here, punk." Sylvester slammed the door shut and locked it, then returned to the dining room.

"What if he doesn't leave?" Adalia murmured, taking her seat again, but her father seemed totally unfazed by the entire encounter.

"He will. He's a coward, my girl. He'll take on an old man because he thinks he has a chance, but you can bet he won't want to mix it up with the cops."

Adalia left her plate untouched and stared dead ahead. "Dad, it's like everything is conspiring against me right now. Wherever I turn, somebody's there to make things more difficult."

Sylvester folded his hands on the table then smoothed the white cloth she'd laid on it earlier in the afternoon. "Nobody has time for a victim. Stop feeling sorry for yourself and get on with it. Figure out what you have to do to make it work. What are you going to do? Curl up in a ball and die?"

"No, of course not," she said, straightening up in the dining room chair. It creaked beneath her. Her dad had had the same set since she was a kid, and she bit her lip.

"Then figure it out, girl. We're here to support you."

"I guess I need to find a way to market the business, get my name out there and bring in more business. But all of that costs money, and that's the one thing I don't have." She pushed her food around on her plate and tapped her cheek with her nail.

"There must be a potential investor you can turn to for help."

She could think of one, but he wouldn't like it.

"I met a billionaire."

"Huh?" Sylvester stopped chewing and placed his fork on the side of his plate. "A billionaire?"

"His name is Trent Dawson. He was a customer of mine, and he invited me to cater at one of his charity events. He's interested in helping others." Her heart beat faster, and she studied her father, leaning her chin on her fist.

"Trent Dawson," he repeated, then shook his head with a sour grunt. "I don't like it, girl."

"What do you mean?"

"Why did this man invite you to an event when he barely knows you?"

"I catered, Dad. Chocolate éclairs." She gritted her teeth then calmed herself. Why did it bother her that he didn't like the sound of Trent?

"He swoops in out of nowhere? I don't like it one bit. He sounds like he's got a hidden agenda. I guarantee it, you take a loan from him and you'll be paying it back for the rest of your natural life." Her father stood and removed his plate then offered to take hers.

"But Dad," she began, passing it over.

"But Dad nothing. Don't you talk to that man again." Sylvester turned and made for the kitchen, as if that was the end of the matter, as if she didn't have a brain or the right to choose for herself.

"You want some apple pie, Dalie?" It was his pet name for her, and had always made her feel the princess.

"Yeah, thanks, Dad."

Adalia stared out the window at the front lawn, which was empty – no DeShawn, thankfully – much like her bank account.

Trent Dawson might have a hidden agenda. Trent Dawson might just want a quick lay.

But what other options did she really have at this point?

She stood and went to help her father whip the cream, but her mind wasn't in it. All she could think of was his arms around her and the soft warmth of his lips on her skin.

Chapter Eight

The bakery was empty except for a student perched in one of the booths in the corner. He had thick glasses and was hunched over his laptop, plugging away at the keys with a danish on his left and a half-empty cup of coffee on his right.

Adalia stood behind the register, enjoying the sunlight on her cheeks. Small pleasures were the key to a happy life.

The kitchen was empty and she'd finished the morning breads and buns hours ago. They were laid out for purchase along with the sweet treats. She stifled a yawn. She'd been up since 2:00am getting everything ready for the day.

She bent her head over her own laptop and surfed the internet, searching for new ways to market, to bring in some kind of business.

The bell over the door rang, but she didn't look up – there was something about social media that called out to her. It might be an easy way to access more clients. Or a Google Business Listing.

"Got any of those cream buns in stock?" Trent spoke directly in front of her. Adalia jumped then cleared her throat.

"Only chocolate," she replied, then pressed her lips together. Trent had that assistant bimbo with him, and a surge of humiliation flooded her. He talked the talk, but he sure didn't walk the walk.

"Sir, are you sure this is the best breakfast choice?" Van Heerden asked, clicking her nails on the counter then bringing out her smart phone to check the time. "There's a health bar a few blocks from here. How about a fruit smoothie?"

"Michelle, when I want your opinion, I'll ask for it." He said it with that cool edge he'd used on Adalia in the kitchen, and she flushed with heat.

This guy was a downright player. He really didn't care about her.

"I'll take a couple of chocolate buns, Adalia."

"Sure," she replied, without a smile and without complaint. The sooner he left, the better. There were too many confusing emotions associated with him. One second she wanted to hold him, the next she wanted to slap him and scream out loud.

It was too much to handle with everything else going on. She hung on by a thread, clinging to sanity for the sake of her strength, for the sake of the business.

Adalia handed him the brown paper bag and he grabbed her by the hand.

"I haven't forgotten." Trent flashed a winning smile.

She gave him a blank stare in return. "I have."

"Excuse me, Ms. Montclair," Van Heerden said, and Adalia turned to the slim blonde. "Do you have anything that isn't pure carbs?"

"I'm sorry, but this is a full fat bakery." Adalia said it with pride, eying the products, packed with calories, gluten and refined sugar. "If you don't like it, I hear there's a health bar a couple blocks away. Why don't you try there?"

"A full fat bakery," Van Heerden said, then paused and looked Adalia up and down, before continuing, "I can tell."

Adalia didn't respond, though her outrage at having the woman pushed into her face had peaked.

"Go wait in the car," Trent said, and Michelle's upper lip curled back.

"Trent," she said, purring his name, caressing it almost. He turned those pools of blue intensity on her. Van Heerden drew her usually pouty lips into a thin line, then spun around and marched out of the bakery. She slammed the glass door hard, but it didn't crack.

"You're a lucky man," Adalia said. "She's a real charmer."

"I'm sorry. I can't account for her behavior. She's been a good assistant, but socially she's totally inept and it's becoming a problem."

"I have no interest in your assistant." Adalia bit her lip and lowered her gaze to the laptop screen again. Trent had chosen today to wear an open-necked shirt without the jacket. The cotton was tight over his torso, and she couldn't handle witnessing the ripples of muscle beneath it. Too tempting.

"But you do have an interest in me." Trent oozed that confidence again, as if he'd never dreamed for a second she might not want him. Unfortunately, he was dead on. She'd love to break that arrogance down a bit, but she was a terrible actor.

"Excuse me, could I get a refill?" the student called out from the corner, and she swept up the pot of coffee and hurried over to help him out. The interruption gave her time to gather herself.

She returned to the counter with a sigh. Trent was still there with his brown paper bag, waiting for her. He didn't check his watch or tap his foot, at least.

"Sorry, you need to pay, don't you?" She rang it up on the cash register and handed him his change.

"At least you let me pay for it this time."

"Yeah, well you did me a favor by letting me cater your event. I figured it was the least I could do," Adalia quipped, and he chuckled. This was nice, it was amicable, and there wasn't pressure to –

"So, I'll pick you up Friday around eight?" Trent placed the bag on the counter, and left it there. The bakery was silent but for the patter of the student's fingers on the keys, and the tension between them heightened.

"What?"

"I told you, Adalia, I always get what I want. You're coming on a date with me on Friday. I won't take no for an answer."

"That's a great pity, because it's the only answer I'm going to give," Adalia grumbled, but she was tired of resisting him.

"Why are you so set on denying this connection? You don't get what's going on here."

"I don't get it? No, you don't. I'm not the kind of woman who deals with men like you on a daily basis. Hell, I don't deal with men like you at all."

"Men like me?" The corners of his mouth twitched in amusement.

The doorbell tinkled again and Michelle pranced in, carrying a smoothie.

"Looks like duty calls," Adalia said, sweet as pie, then picked up his brown paper bag and shoved it at him.

He didn't take the bag, but let it slide back to the counter. The really strange version of pass the parcel continued.

Michelle stopped beside them and slurped on the straw, pursing her lips in the most obvious way. She was built to seek attention, from her dyed roots to her revealing top to her stiletto heels.

"I thought I told you to wait in the car." A muscle twitched in Trent's jaw. He probably didn't want her to know he'd propositioned Adalia, the creep.

"I got bored," she replied with a shrug.

"Have a nice day, Mr. Dawson," Adalia put in, by way of a dismissal. She'd had enough of his games and there was business to attend to.

"Give me your number," he said, with a straight face.

Michelle's eyebrows flickered upward.

Adalia opened her mouth to snap at him. He didn't know when to quit, but the doorbell rang again and she rammed her mouth shut.

"Hey, baby." DeShawn strolled in with his usual swagger, the gangster limp he'd adopted on the streets.

"Baby?" Trent's head swiveled from DeShawn to Adalia. "You can't be serious."

DeShawn stopped in front of the cash register and adjusted his do-rag, then scratched his crotch. Michelle's mouth turned downward, and she gave a sniff of disdain.

"What up, girl?"

Chapter Nine

"What are you doing here, DeShawn?" Adalia took in even breaths, stilling the sudden swell of anxiety in the pit of her stomach.

It was obvious why her ex was there. To hunt her down, cause trouble and exact whatever price he desired.

"I've had enough of this. I told you not to come back here again," Adalia hissed at him, but it was no use – even the student in the far booth had perked up at her ex-boyfriend's entrance.

"I ain't ever gonna give up on what we had." He scratched at his nose with his thumb and sniffed hard.

"You'll have to, because I'm never taking you back."

DeShawn side-eyed Michelle and then Trent, then gave a short burst of laughter. "Take me back? Bitch, please, I dumped your ass."

"Maybe in imaginary land," she said, stifling a snort of disbelief. The cheek of this guy was beyond comprehension, but she should've expected no less from him. He was unfathomable to her, as were his motivations, unless of course you counted smoking pot and drinking. Those two were the most obvious.

Otherwise he was a mystery. And not the Trent Dawson kind, no, more like the kind you didn't want to find out more about because you were too afraid of what you'd find when you popped the lid on the gangster-appareled box.

Adalia searched the room for some escape and the bell over the door chimed again. Her heart pounded in her chest, but it was just one of her regulars, not another remnant from the past.

"Hello, dearie. I've come for more of those fantastic chocolate éclairs."

"Of course, Mrs. Greene, right away," Adalia answered with a relieved smile and hurried to fulfill the order. Anything to be away from the melting pot of tension waiting to explode.

She carefully boxed the éclairs, taking extra time to create the cut-out cardboard casing herself. DeShawn and Trent stood nearby, staring at her, observing her every move. It was the most awkward experience of her life.

"Here you go, Mrs. Greene," she said, passing her the white and pink cardboard construction.

"Thank you, dear," Mrs.Greene murmured, then tapped the side of her nose with a wink. "I would stay to chat, but it looks like you've got enough company at the moment." She shuffled out in her favorite slippers, curlers still tangled in the plum-colored strands of her graying hair.

Adalia longed to call out after her to stay, please God, stay and chat, but she didn't. Instead, she walked back to her place at the laptop and browsed the Internet.

"Are you gonna talk to me about it?" DeShawn rammed his knuckles onto the counter.

"This guy giving you trouble, Adalia?" Trent asked, stepping forward and rolling up his sleeves to reveal defined forearms covered in a fine coating of blond hair.

"Who the hell are you?" DeShawn asked.

"I'm the last man you'll ever see, that's who the hell I am." Trent flashed his even, white teeth.

"There's too much testosterone in the air," Adalia said and Michelle actually nodded in agreement. Their gazes met for a second and then flinched away from each other.

"I don't got time for you, boy, you'd better watch your ass before I break it for you."

"Sorry," Trent said with a chuckle, "but I'm not into guys."

"Aw, you think you're funny, right?" DeShawn reached around the waistband of his jeans, and Adalia slapped her hand on the counter hard.

"Don't you even think of doing what you're about to, DeShawn. I'll make you regret it." She couldn't keep the panic from her tone, but it still stopped him from drawing his gun in her bakery.

That stupid pistol. She hated it with all the parts of her soul. She'd never forget the day he came home with it and stood in the kitchen in a drug-induced stupor, waving the thing around like a mafia boss on crack.

DeShawn froze and slowly pulled his hand back round to the front. "You expect me to stand down to this punk?" He pointed at Trent, who cocked his head to the side and squared his shoulders.

"I expect you to get the hell out of my bakery." Adalia picked up her cell and started dialing.

"What are you doing?" DeShawn asked with a hint of fear.

"Calling the cops. You'd better get out of here, now."

"You wouldn't do that," he said, denying it with a low, stupid giggle.

"Hi, yes, I've got an armed individual in my bakery." She paused and listened hard. "A pistol, yes. He's threatening my customers. I have his name and address, too, if you –"

"Aight, aight, I'm going, just hang up the phone, girl." DeShawn backed off until his back hit the door. He grappled with the handle behind him, then swung it open and slunk through it.

Adalia placed the phone on the counter again. She'd called her home number, not the cops, but it worked like a charm every time. DeShawn definitely wasn't the brightest cookie in the jar.

"That's your ex-boyfriend." Trent watched him saunter off, without a backward glance. "You chose that guy?"

"How about you leave, too, before I make another call," she said, laying her hand on the cell again.

He smirked at her. "And what, tell the fake police I'm intruding on your personal space? Get real, Adalia."

"I have no interest in talking to you, Trent. You've been nothing but trouble since the minute you walked into this bakery."

"Yes, because hiring you was trouble for you."

"I didn't ask for your charity, and I certainly don't need it. Now, get out!" Adalia closed the lid of her laptop with too much force, but she couldn't control the red hot rage pumping through her veins.

Trent Dawson glared at her, spearing her with daggers of his anger. "Don't ever speak to me like that again."

Then he left, closing the door behind him without force. He was in control, every movement measured to avoid rash actions. He was the opposite of DeShawn, but he was just as bad. Wasn't he?

"You're so dumb," Michelle Van Heerden said, slurping on that damn smoothie with relish.

"Huh?"

"Trent Dawson is interested in you and you kick him out of your insignificant bakery? You're so stupid. So, so, so stupid." Michelle pronounced each 'so' with absolute clarity.

"You can get out, too," Adalia hissed.

"Oh, I will, gladly. Fortunately I don't eat carbs, or I'd end up looking like you. Yuk." She ambled off a few feet, those stilettos biting at the linoleum, but stopped and looked back. "You stay away from Trent. I've worked too long and too hard to get him into bed and I won't let you stand in my way."

Did that mean she wasn't his girlfriend?

"I would have thought you'd have managed it already, what with all the experience you have in that department." It wasn't thinly veiled, but an insult in its purest form.

But Michelle seemed oblivious. She popped her hip and pouted. "I know, right? But he's weirdly allergic to my charms or something. Anyway, just stay away from him if you know what's good for you."

She disappeared with another ring of the bell.

Adalia slumped into the cushy chair she'd positioned behind the counter for moments like these. Trent wasn't involved with Michelle and she'd yelled at him, forced him out of her shop.

She slapped her forehead hard. The one guy she'd found unbelievably attractive, the one guy she thought she couldn't have, was never with Michelle.

And she'd embarrassed him in front of his assistant and another patron.

What was the matter with her?

Maybe she just wasn't cut out for the whole dating scene. Adalia glanced up and ground her teeth at the memory of Michelle's threat.

One thing was for sure… there was no backing down now.

If Trent asked her again, the answer would be a resounding 'yes'.

Chapter Ten

"I thought you'd appreciate this atmosphere." Trent gestured to the sultry candlelight in the romantic French restaurant off main. "It seemed you needed the silence."

"You got that right," Adalia sighed and took a long drink from the champagne flute. She'd agreed to the date out of anger at Michelle, but she truly wanted to be there. She wanted to know him, even though she still wasn't sure she could trust him.

"Care to discuss it?" He took a sip of his own champagne, and the flute looked undersized in his strong hands. She pictured the stem snapping and a thrill passed over her.

"There's no point. I can handle it."

"You don't have to be this strong all the time. You're allowed to accept help from others, you know. You're allowed to be vulnerable sometimes." The words passed his lips as a mantra, but it wasn't the first time she'd heard them.

It didn't matter. She was determined to do what was best for the bakery, and that meant handling it on her own. She'd trusted DeShawn and where had that gotten her? In debt, that was where.

Adalia sighed and sat back in the cream-upholstered chair of dark wood, trying to soak up the gentle ambience, the soft music of violins in the background.

"So you don't want to talk about your business," he said, taking a bread roll from the basket and placing it on his side plate.

"No," she answered, a little too firmly.

Trent nodded, cut the roll open and buttered it with care. "And you don't want to talk about your personal life."

"No," she said, scrunching the napkin in her lip. It was of the finest cotton, and embroidered, too.

"Then, gorgeous, what do you want to talk about?" He took a bite of the roll and grinned at her. "The crisis in the Middle East?"

Adalia laughed at that. His warmth was infectious and it was a nice change from his continuous 'hunt' mode where he dominated her.

"How about we talk about you, Mr. Mysterious?" She took a roll and buttered it as well, and was treated to a sexy lopsided smile from Trent.

"That's Sir Mysterious to you, young lady." He paused and finished chewing, then took some more champagne. "And you'll never believe what I do, anyway."

Adalia sat back with the dinner roll in hand. "Humor me."

"All right, but don't say I didn't warn you."

A waiter arrived with their entrées and they ate thoughtfully, forks and knives clinking softly against their plates. Trent still managed the story.

"I fly people to the moon."

"What?" Adalia coughed into her napkin in the most ladylike way possible.

He chuckled and dabbed at the corners of his mouth. "I've always been into aviation, and my company is responsible for building ships that take tourists to the moon. Basically, chartered holidays. It's a once in a lifetime opportunity and its set to launch soon.

Our only real competition is SkyLyft, but after their most recent disaster, we're the favorites."

"Are you serious?"

"It's the same as any other trip. Think of it as a holiday."

"To the moon," she said, in disbelief. Here she was, worrying about her bakery on little old Earth, and Trent Dawson was on his way to the heavens. It suited him, though it grated on her to admit it.

He probably hadn't worked a day in his life. He'd been born rich, gotten all the resources he needed to get ahead in life and here he was.

"That's correct. I told you it's pretty unbelievable."

"I think it's fascinating," she said, fluttering her eyelids at him then turning away in embarrassment. It was impossible that she was this drawn in by him. One meal and she was moments from throwing herself across the table.

Trent stood and gestured to a waiter.

"Are you full?" Adalia frowned, dropping her fork and grasping her handbag. DeShawn had always left restaurants when he was done eating, regardless of how far she was into her meal.

"No way," he replied then picked up his chair and shifted it to her side. The waiter moved his plate and champagne glass, though looked seriously uncomfortable that Trent had moved his own chair.

The maître d' hovered in the background, shooting dirty looks at the poor aproned guy.

Trent grabbed their waiter's arm and leaned in close. "You tell that guy that if he looks for trouble with you, I'll buy this place and fire him."

The waiter gave a small yelp and hurried away, giving the maître d' a wide berth regardless. Trent settled into his chair beside her and grasped her hand in his. Fingers of doubt and need crawled up her spine, massaging tension in and out of her muscles. She wanted him, she craved him, but she was sure it was wrong.

"I thought you and Michelle were an item," she popped it out without warning, even to herself.

"In her wildest dreams. Michelle's a good assistant but she's about as bright as a clam and excites me about as much."

She leaned back, straining that invisible cord of desire between them with distance. "That's a bit harsh."

"I say it how it is. I didn't get ahead by playing nice." Trent was matter of fact and even though his arrogance had surpassed peak levels, she was still drawn to him. To that special brand of real power and panache.

That was her thing, obviously. DeShawn had seemed a boss, in control and cool. She'd seen him as a real man in the beginning, but Trent had changed her perception of what a real man was.

"You've gone quiet," he said, stroking her skin with his thumb, then he stopped and let go of her. "I'm not usually like this. I know what I want and I get it."

"I thought that was what this was."

"You don't understand, gorgeous," he whispered, tracing the line of her neck and down to her chest with the back of his index finger. He halted short of her breasts then retraced his caress again. "What I want is usually a one night stand. A quick fuck so that I won't be exposed to any emotional connection with a woman who's clearly not in my league."

"Wow," she replied, shaking her head, "just wow. You've got a rather large opinion of yourself, Dawson."

"I'm being honest, Adalia."

"So am I. Don't for a second think you'll ever get that from me." She laughed at herself and shifted her chair away. "I was such an asshole to come here with you after that whole fake speech about not wanting a conquest."

"Quiet. Let me finish."

But she wouldn't. "I've got news for you, Mr. Dawson, you will never get me. Conquest away, wine and dine me, pretend to be something you're not, but you will never –"

Trent reeled that cord in, by placing his hand around the back of her neck. He brought his lips to hers and parted them, slipping his tongue inside her mouth to taste her. He was sweet with a hint of champagne.

She moaned into him and he gripped her tighter, running his fingers down her cheek and resting them on her chin, tilting her head back as he liked. She was putty in his hands. He could mold her however he wanted and she wouldn't care.

All bravado ceased to exist. Adalia was his; he merely had to tell her so.

They broke apart and he poked her gently on the nose. "You were saying, Ms. Montclair?"

"Your place or mine?"

Chapter Eleven

"So, this is where you live." Trent strolled into her tiny living room, hands in his pockets, bulging muscles in every damn direction.

Adalia closed the door behind them, sauntering to the kitchen to take out another bottle of wine. She'd had too much already, but she hadn't let loose in weeks, so what the hell. What was the harm in having a little fun?

She turned back to Trent and the wine glasses fell from her hand and shattered on the floor.

He was topless in the middle of the living room. His abs rippled under the harsh lighting.

"W-what are you doing?" She placed the wine bottle on the counter behind her without looking away.

"Come here," he said, by way of an answer. She stepped out of her shoes and tiptoed to him, a fire burning in her soul, holding vigil for what was about to happen.

She was a one-night stand to him. She couldn't let this happen!

Adalia's feet slowed, and she jolted to a halt.

"Now."

They started moving again. She couldn't resist that command and the underlying tension caused by his intense need for her.

He needed her, she could tell. She could see it in those bright blue eyes, could practically smell the pheromones in the air.

She wanted nothing more than to please him, than to make him see she was more than just another woman. A conquest to put in the memory bank for examination, but a woman who deserved more, who deserved his respect.

All of these desires, conflicting, swirling around in her brain creating a true belief that maybe, just maybe, he'd want it with her. The real thing she'd never had but dreamed about. Hell, what every girl in the world dreamed about.

"Faster. I need you."

That phrase was her poison. Her nightshade. It would be her undoing, and she'd let him remake her in the image he wanted. But only for the night. She wasn't weak, but she did deserve this.

Hadn't she worked hard enough?

Moments became hours in her existence, stretching out into an eternity of him there in the living room, half naked, mere feet from her, waiting for her to come to him. Hours of her tiptoeing, stepping so carefully, so he'd see how much this meant to her.

Then it was over. She was in front of him and he loomed above her, looking down at the top of her head, unyielding and strong.

She touched his abs and ran her hands up his chest and looped her arms around his neck, then let out a soft moan.

"You want me."

She swallowed several times, biting her lip and staring into his eyes.

"Say it. Say you want me, Adalia."

She gasped at the sound of her name on his lips. "I want you."

"Good. Don't ever forget it."

Adalia had no words left, and she wasn't sure she had actions either. She was glued to him, trapped in the forever of the moment with him.

He reached around and laid one hand on her ass, gripping it with a low guttural groan of pleasure. That noise, the idea that he was this attracted to her, sent her into overdrive.

"Trent, please," she whispered, and he looked into her eyes, searching her soul for the question she was about to ask. "Kiss me."

He tucked that hand beneath her ass and used his other arm to catch her back. He lifted her from the floor and carried her to the couch, then laid her on it, ever so gently, as if she was his treasure.

Trent lay down on top of her, distributing his weight evenly on either forearm, braced against her couch.

He kissed her gently, then parted her lips with his tongue and tasted her in earnest, probing and savoring her. She followed his lead, enjoying the pressure of his kiss. He pressed himself against her, grinding until she shifted her legs and wrapped them around his waist, angling herself upward to rub against him.

He growled and stroked her hair while they made out, then he slid that hand down and cupped her breast, stroking it in circles.

Trent pulled back from the kiss and she grasped his neck, willing him to come back down to her.

He grinned, that same sly half-smile he'd melted her with in the restaurant then unbuttoned her blouse. She gasped and he took both of her breasts out, pressed them together and lowered his head to tickle her nipples with the tip of his tongue.

He took both of them into his mouth simultaneously and sucked hard, pulling them upward. The wet sensation of his tongue licking and sucking her drove her over the edge.

"Oh God, I want you. I need you inside me," she whispered, and he nibbled on her breasts. "Please," she begged. "Trent, please, I have to have you now."

"Not yet," he said, around a mouthful of her breast. "Not until I'm done." He forced his hand down her skirt and into her lacy hot panties, searching for her wetness. He found it, and she arched her back.

"That's my girl," he uttered, working her clit with one finger, circling it at first then tapping instead.

She cried out in pleasure, moving past the present and into some other world with him, another time where they were the only ones that existed. The only ones who mattered.

"Come on, Adalia, you're all mine, I want you to come for me."

She gripped at his arms, his head, any bit of skin she could get at. She needed an anchor. The first waves of pleasure came in rapid succession, crashing over her, and her body convulsed against him.

"That's it. You're all mine," he grunted, pressing his massive erection against her as she trembled from the intensity of her orgasm.

"Trent, stop. I want you inside me now."

"No, you're going to come for me, Adalia." He was insistent, and he played with her, dipping his fingers inside her and stroking her G-spot with his two fingers. The pressure built, and he used his other hand to play with her clit. He worked them together, in a perfect rhythm. She couldn't hold on for any longer.

"I'm going to –"

"You're my woman." He slowed his fingers and kissed her cheeks, then her eyelids, then the tip of her nose.

"Oh God," she said, gasping for breath after the tremors finally abated. "Trent, that was unbelievable."

"Don't you worry, we're not done yet," he said, standing and unzipping his pants. He reached in and –

Crash!

Her front door slammed open, and DeShawn stood framed in the doorway, swaying from side-to-side in a drunken stupor.

Trent froze, rage spreading through his muscles in a visible ripple. He zipped up his tailored pants and glared at her ex-boyfriend. This was a disaster.

If DeShawn got out of hand and Trent got sick of it, there'd be a massive blowout.

"Hey, baby!" DeShawn stumbled in a few feet then noticed Trent.

"No!" Adalia yelled. "Get out of my apartment!"

"What the fuck's going on here?"

Chapter Twelve

"Get out of my apartment!" Adalia sprang into the upright position and shimmied off the couch. She covered herself up and DeShawn stumbled back and forth, eyes marred by a red haze – drugs, obviously.

"You heard her," Trent growled, but her ex-boyfriend didn't turn away. "Get out of here."

"You get outta here, man," DeShawn slurred then straightened. There was an iron rod between his shoulders, a bar of tension that spelled danger.

Adalia had seen that stance before – she'd witnessed DeShawn beat a guy to a near pulp for saying the wrong thing. He was built like a bulldog, and even more ferocious when he was intoxicated.

"Calm down," Adalia said, and both men shot her a look of venom. They wanted her to butt out of it, but she wouldn't let them fight over her. This was ridiculous. "I have work tomorrow, I've got a business to run, and I don't have time for this, guys."

"You don't have time to kick your ex out of your apartment? How did he even get in here?" Trent's jaw was clenched tight.

Adalia studied the closed lid of her laptop, tracing the lines of its rounded edges and avoiding the question.

"You ain't gonna answer that, baby?" DeShawn chuckled, then squared those broad shoulders again and nearly lost his balance.

"Clown," Trent replied.

"Don't start something you can't finish, boy," DeShawn snapped.

"How did he get in here?" Trent repeated, but Adalia didn't want to admit this to him. She didn't want him to see her for the weakness she still had within. She wasn't a failure, she wasn't!

"Adalia, you need to tell me this, right now." Trent was buckled up, his shirt was open and he took the moment to button it back up.

"He has a key."

"What? Why?"

"I never took it back from him. I tried, but he wouldn't give it back to me."

"So you just gave up? You knew he had access to your place and you just stopped trying to get it back from him? What did you think was going to happen?"

"She wanted me to come for her, man. This bitch needs me." DeShawn grinned, flashing those skew teeth at the pair of them.

"Don't call her that," Trent warned, raising a fist and glaring at her ex with a gaze of liquefied fire. There was so much anger in him, and she'd not seen it there before.

"Both of you stop this, it's pointless."

"I had no idea you were still connected to this loser. I mean, I should've realized the minute he walked into your bakery and started throwing his ghetto weight around, but this is fucking ridiculous."

"Stop, Trent, please just stop." She'd never expressed this much weakness before. Except when she'd allowed DeShawn to do what he liked, when he liked.

"I miss living here, baby, I think it's time we get together again."

"Living here?" Trent's eyes became saucers then narrowed a second later. "You lived with this fool?"

"Yes," she said, then walked to the kitchen and poured herself a glass of water. She swallowed it in a few massive gulps then stared at them across the counter. She didn't need this level of stress.

She should've gone with her initial instincts. Trent was trouble, and he cared more about conquests and fulfilling his ego than he did about her, that much was plain.

"You don't even care about what's going on here," Trent growled.

"I don't care about being judged by you, when it's clear to me you were only ever interested in one thing. You got what you wanted, Dawson, now you can leave my apartment and never come back." She put on the hardness she wore as a shell during times of strife. Her dad had taught her that trick.

She could handle this. She didn't need help or support. She didn't need interference.

"You're unbelievable." Trent shook his head then ran a hand through his short blond hair. "I thought we had something special here."

"That's your line, Trent, but I'm not stupid. I don't want either of you in my apartment or my life."

"Don't say that, baby, you know you miss us." DeShawn swayed slightly.

"Like a heart attack," she replied, then slapped the glass into the sink and rinsed it out.

"I can't believe you were with this loser." Trent's entire body trembled with anger, and a patchwork of redness spread up his neck. Anger? He was angry? Poor little rich man, angry because he couldn't get his way.

She had to degrade him.

DeShawn gripped the doorjamb and pushed himself further into her living room. "You wanna take this outside?"

"Shut up," Trent barked. "I'm in the middle of a conversation."

"Now it's on," DeShawn said, bulleting forward another five steps. He was within arm's reach of Trent and Adalia squeezed her eyes shut for a millisecond, willing her anxiety to abate.

DeShawn threw his fists up and Trent left his at his sides, a wry smile spreading across his face. His eyes were half-crazed, wide and intimidating, but DeShawn didn't notice them. He was too drunk.

"Trent, don't hurt him."

The billionaire raised a hand and pressed it into DeShawn's face, then shoved him back with such force that he spun on the spot. The hood rat careened backward.

Crash!

He fell onto the chair she'd placed beside her front door to hold her mail. It splintered into pieces, sending shards of wood in every direction.

"Don't defend him." Trent pointed to DeShawn.

"You broke my chair," she replied with a blank expression. "It was the only other one I had."

"Don't you ever defend him again. He's nothing. He's nothing to you." Trent pointed at DeShawn then back at her. He moved past the sofa where they'd shared passion for an eternity, and approached the counter. "Don't talk about him like he matters."

"Of course he matters. He's part of my past."

"I can't accept you would be with a man who would treat you that way."

"And I can't accept you'd use me for sex but, hey, we all have baggage to bear, right?" Adalia picked up the glass again, and he grabbed it from her and slammed it down in the sink.

"Don't talk to me like that. Don't talk to me about baggage."

"Stop telling me what to do," she muttered. That intense need to touch him built up again and she forced it aside. What the hell was wrong with her?

DeShawn groaned on the floor nearby.

"You broke my chair," Adalia said.

Trent cracked his knuckles. "Relax. I'll buy you another fucking chair."

"Don't bother, just take him and get out of here."

"I'm not touching him, Adalia. He's your problem. You wanted to get involved with a man like that, and this is what comes of it." Trent's rage definitely hadn't dissipated. He stretched his neck until it cracked.

"That's fine." Adalia pretended it didn't hurt. She was strong. She could do it all on her own. She had before and she would again. She didn't need anyone for anything!

"You don't care about anyone but yourself," Trent snapped.

"Get out of my apartment."

Trent braced himself with both hands on the counter, straining against it and her. "You sure about this, Adalia? It might be the last you see of me."

"Get out."

He turned and stormed to the door, then paused and looked down on DeShawn, who was groaning under his breath. Trent bent down, grabbed DeShawn by the front of his shirt and dragged him out into the hall.

He bent over the downed wannabe gangsta and fumbled in his pockets. He brought out Adalia's keys and threw them into the apartment. Then he marched off down the hall without a goodbye.

Adalia locked the door.

Chapter Thirteen

Adalia stared at the page of text, fingers tracing the words again and again. It was the second warning from the bank. She had a week now, one week and they'd take the business for collateral damage.

The cash register was in front of her, the bakery was empty as usual and she was alone.

There was no fragrant aroma of baking chocolate buns or croissants. There were no cupcakes to be iced. Even her regular, the old lady, hadn't come in for her éclairs.

There wasn't money for marketing, and even if she marketed and brought in more customers, there wouldn't be money to hire help to fulfill those orders.

How had it come to this?

She'd started with hopes and grand dreams. She'd envisioned an empire for the family, a legacy for her children if she ever had any. Adalia snorted, not that she'd ever have time for that or a man worthy of being a father to them.

"This is the end," she whispered to herself, then slid the paper to the side of the register. She opened it up and glared at the lack of money. "This is what it's come to."

There weren't any breaks.

She needed a loan to kick start the business, but she couldn't afford to pay off the last one. Had she spent unwisely?

Adalia slapped the drawer closed. She was so tired of doubting herself about this! She'd tried damn hard to make it work, but it was never enough.

The bell over the door tinkled and she blinked, hope erupting outward with each beat of her heart.

It crashed down around her ears. Nope, not a customer.

"What are you doing here?" She turned her back on Trent, swept up her duster and reached for the shelves behind her. She'd stacked empty biscuit tins, vintage of course, up there for decoration and they gathered a shocking amount of dust.

Not that any of it mattered now.

"We need to talk about what happened."

"No, we really don't." Adalia continued dusting, sweeping the feathers over her tins gently. She'd put so much care into this place, so much love and care because it was her dream. Her true passion and it was about to be snatched away because she couldn't make it work.

It wasn't anyone's fault but hers, and that stung the most. She couldn't make it work. She had failed.

No, it wasn't over yet. There had to be a way to solve this.

Trent cleared his throat but she ignored it and placed the duster beneath the counter.

"What's this?"

She frowned and turned to him, then froze. Shame colored her cheeks and she rubbed them, then reached over and snatched the notice from the bank out of his grip.

"Mind your own business."

"Looks like you need to mind yours," he answered, but his tone was peppered with concern rather than disdain. "Adalia, I want to see you succeed at this, and I can't deny that I'm worried."

"I don't need your concern or your pity. I've never needed it and what happens in my life is truly none of your business," she said, forcing her palm toward him. "Back off."

He grabbed her and pulled her closer, bending her over the counter so his nose was against hers. "I'll never back off. I never back down when I want something."

"You got what you wanted the other night."

"What are you talking about?" He released her and walked to one of the tables. He lowered himself into a chair and folded his hands on the surface.

There was hardly any traffic on the road outside, but for a stray car every few minutes. An old Mazda puttered down the road, breaking the tension between them and settling a layer of comfort over their conversation.

"I don't want to discuss this with you, Trent. I'm over it. I'm over you, too." Blatant lie, but what the hell. She had to get him out and it was the only way to do that.

"What are you talking about?"

Adalia clicked over on the anger meter. "You wanted sex from me, you wanted a conquest and you got it. You didn't even have the damn courtesy to walk out of there without hurling insults and judgment. I don't need that in my life."

She judged herself enough for the both of them.

"That's what you really think." Trent sighed, shoulders shifting up and down under that suit. Armani again? "I told you I want you for you, for more than just a conquest. I'm not that kind of guy, Adalia."

"I don't care what you say." She denied tears. She wouldn't feel sorry for herself over this! She'd been fooled and that was that.

Trent rose and walked around to her side of the counter. She took a few steps back to distance herself, but he rushed forward and pressed her up against the wall.

"I want you for you, not for your body or your mind, or any single part of you. I have no agendas."

"Right," she breathed, rolling her eyes and resisting the urge to bite his lip.

"I want what's best for you. I want you to succeed."

"Why?"

"Because I care about you," he whispered, brow wrinkling then smoothing again. "How can you not know that?"

She slid her hands up his chest and rested them on those defined pecs, than gave a tiny moan. He was so delicious. A white chocolate treat and she'd unwrap him and gobble him up if she got the chance.

Adalia pushed him back and he let go, then leaned against the hip-height counter.

"What's going on here?" Trent gestured to the bakery, and she gave a mighty sigh. She still wasn't sure of him yet, but she needed to talk.

"The bank's going to take it away because I can't pay off my loan, and I don't have any customers."

"Maybe you just haven't put yourself out there enough. What's your marketing budget?"

"I don't have one. I used every cent I got setting this place up and even if I could market, I wouldn't be able to supply new customers with enough products to meet their demand because I can't afford to hire any help."

Poor Jenny, she missed that girl. She'd been such a help in times of trouble. She'd been with her from the start. And now it was the end.

"So get another loan."

"How am I supposed to get another loan when I can't even pay off the last one?"

"I'll loan you the money." Trent paused then spread his arms wide, as if he expected a hug. "Hell, I'll even give it to you, no catch. Totally obligation free."

Adalia stared at him long and hard. She didn't consider the proposition - that was out of the question - but she had to take him in. He thought he could throw money at any problem and it would go away, probably because that's how he was raised.

"No thank you," she replied, with too much curtness.

"Why not? You need the help, and I'm willing to offer it."

"I'm fine, thanks. I don't need your money." A slow burn had started in her belly.

"I think you do," he answered, motioning to the empty room.

"I don't want or need your money, Dawson. Everything I have, I worked for, and I don't take handouts." She straightened and folded her arms. "Unlike you."

"Excuse me?"

"I don't take handouts. I'm sure you're used to them, but I'm not. I have some dignity left." Adalia smirked, even though she didn't find any of this amusing.

"I'll see you around." Trent didn't argue, but an expression of pain – not anger – flashed across his face.

The bell over the door tinkled to signal his departure.

Chapter Fourteen

"I'm sorry," said Adalia, pressing the receiver to her ear and breathing lightly. She didn't want to let on how freaked out she was.

She'd been too harsh the day before, probably because she was jealous of his success on some level. Jealousy was never constructive, anyway.

"That's okay." Trent coughed away from the phone then cleared his throat. "I understand you're going through a tough time. Sorry if I came on too strong."

"No, that's all right. I was a bitch on wheels yesterday." Adalia smiled in spite of the situation. She shifted around on her sofa, unable to banish the flash to Trent on top of her. It made her squirm.

"Look, I've gotta run. I'll catch up with you later."

The phone line went dead, and Adalia sighed softly. That was it. Trent was definitely finished with her, and that was the way it was supposed to be. She didn't really have time for complications.

She swept a tear from under her eyelid and flicked it away.

Maybe if she tried social media marketing, or printed out some flyers, things would pick up. She rose from the sofa and strolled to the kitchen, then took out a wine glass and a bottle of red from the cupboard.

She poured it and took a sip, then settled back into place in front of her laptop. She passed a half hour creating an account for the bakery on Twitter. She probably should've put one up before, but she hadn't had the time.

There was a knock at the door.

Adalia frowned, set the wine glass down and went to answer it. This had better not be DeShawn.

She opened up and gasped.

"Would you care to accompany me to dinner?" Trent stood before her in a tailored suit with a cheesy grin and a bouquet of red roses.

She took them, blinking and pressing down the sudden excitement bouncing around in her stomach.

"Thank you," she breathed.

"I had to come. I wanted us to have a real talk, not one where either of us is stressed out." Trent glanced at the keys on the wall beside the door.

"I – I think that's a good idea. Just give me a minute to put these in water." She was overwhelmed, caught off guard, and that deep need for him was back in the center of her chest, just beside her heart.

Adalia fumbled the roses into a vase with water and positioned it carefully on the kitchen counter. He didn't creep up behind her and pin her to it for a change, but stood patiently at the door.

Trent held it open for her, then closed it and checked it was locked, before escorting her down to his waiting Audi. He opened the door and she slid into the passenger seat then buckled herself in.

They rode in total silence, sparks flying between them. She couldn't tear her eyes from his strong hands on the wheel, from the power he possessed when he changed gears and took corners.

He gave the keys to the valet with a wink and helped her out of the car. He didn't let anyone touch her, open the door. He didn't let them near and she loved it.

They were seated in the low lit room, with a candle flickering on the table between them. Trent shifted it aside and took hold of her hand with a smile that melted her to the core.

There were happy couples dining around them, beside the round tables with pristine white table cloths and flawless silverware atop them.

"I'm glad we'll get this chance to talk."

"Could you have chosen a more romantic restaurant?" Adalia bit her lip.

He chuckled at her. "I couldn't help myself. I've been dying to get you alone and have a real talk."

"We've had real talks."

"No, we've had real fights. There's a difference." He picked up a champagne flute and she clinked hers against it. They both drank the contents down in one go, nervous or just in need of a buzz to smooth the evening's flow.

"You wanted to talk to me?" Adalia prompted, placing the glass to her left and stroking his thumb with hers. She couldn't help herself. She wanted him to feel the passion she held in her heart.

And it was all for him.

It didn't matter what had happened in the past, or the problems she had at that very minute, the only thing which mattered was them. This moment, this feeling. It was everything to her, and she had to have it be everything to him.

"Adalia, I can't stop thinking of you. You're consuming my every thought. It's kinda making it difficult to work," he joked, but she didn't laugh.

Emotion sat in the center of her forehead, and she gazed into his soul. Needing the truth. Please, God, let this man want her. Let him truly need her the way she desired him.

"I…" She trailed off and blew out a breath.

"Come on. Relax. I'm not going to hurt you or trick you, because the only thing I want is your happiness. And mine, too, of course. I'd love it if they coincided."

"I can't stop thinking of you either. Sitting on that sofa is torture."

Trent grasped her other hand, threw back his head and gave a laugh of the purest delight.

"I'm glad that you're in the same boat as me, at least in one way."

"What do you mean?"

Trent grew serious, releasing her and smoothing the table cloth, brow creasing. Forks and knives scratched on plates in the background, and the low chatter of the other diners punctuated his silence.

"You need financial help for your business and I can provide it."

"I told you I don't take handouts," she said, anger building in place of the comfortable buzz of the champagne and the soft glow of his affection.

"I understand that, but something you said alarmed me."

Adalia swallowed hard. She had to calm down. She couldn't ruin this moment with him over her pride and need for independence. "What was it?"

Trent smoothed the cloth again, then picked up his napkin and dabbed at his mouth. He was never this self-conscious. "I never had a handout in life. I worked for everything I have."

Music played alongside his words. Hozier, something soulful and bluesy, and it suited the ambience perfectly. She swayed in time to it in spite of the gravity of the situation. "What?"

"I worked for my money. I didn't get anything from my parents. I started out with a business plan and a loan. I worked at Starbucks at the time, and I didn't want to be a loser anymore. I saw there was a future for what I wanted to do."

"Did you have a college degree?"

"Yeah, but I had a student loan to pay off and I had it nearly done from working as one of those damn baristas."

Adalia clenched her jaw against the flush of embarrassment. She was worse than DeShawn. She'd made a spot judgement about him and rolled with it, not bothering to check if she had it right or not.

It was despicable.

"I'm so sor –"

"Mr. Dawson," a woman spoke up, "fancy meeting you here." Michelle Van Heerden strolled up to their table with a muscled young man in tow. She ignored her date and placed her manicured nails on the back of Trent's neck.

He frowned up at her. "I thought I told you to work on that proposal tonight. What are you doing here?" But he didn't shrug off her touch.

"Just taking a break, sir." the skinny assistant replied, then flashed a triumphant look at Adalia.

Chapter Fifteen

"Thanks for stopping by," Adalia said, glaring up at Michelle with a forced smile. It was her 'fuck you' smile and it showed the danger she had in her.

Adalia was not a pushover – not anymore, at least.

The hot guy folded his arms and then dropped them down to his side, giving Michelle a sidelong glance. "We gonna sit down and get some dinner or what, babe?"

"In a minute," she snapped, not removing her hand from the back of Trent's neck.

Trent finally moved away from her, shifting in his chair to glare. "What do you want, Michelle?"

"Oh, nothing in particular. I just thought we'd say hello."

"You've said hello. Now, leave us in peace." Trent took up his refilled glass and sipped from it. "We're in the middle of a private conversation."

"Of course, but I thought I'd let you know that Mr. Harrington called about commissioning the new shuttle for its trial run." Michelle picked an invisible speck of dirt off her bright red silk mini-dress.

Adalia repressed the urge to slap her.

Trent perked up and put down the glass. "Mr. Harrington? What did he say?"

"He suggested you call him immediately. I believe it's important, sir," she whispered, bending over to display her fake cleavage. Her date was captivated by her ass and Adalia rolled her eyes.

"Why didn't you phone me?"

"I tried, sir, but you didn't answer," Michelle murmured, hair hanging as a curtain in front of her face. Adalia folded her hands on the table and waited patiently. Work was work, but it was so obvious that Michelle had planned this.

Maybe she'd known he'd be here; she was his assistant after all.

Trent looked over at Adalia and studied her.

"It's okay, do what you have to do. I totally understand," she said, before he could bring out the question or apology.

"Thanks," he replied, then took up her hand and brushed his lips across the back of it. The sensation was soft and warm, but Adalia's insides had turned cold at the sight of that woman.

Michelle straightened and waited for Trent to rise. He did so, brought out his phone and excused himself. Adalia didn't watch him go, but focused on his tall assistant instead: she hadn't excused herself yet.

"Hun, could you get me a spritzer at the bar? I'll meet you there."

"Thought we were gonna blow this joint after you spoke to the boss man," the trophy boy replied, and Michelle wrapped her arms around him and pressed her chest against his. He stammered wordlessly.

"Just get me a spritzer, darling, and I promise I'll blow whatever you like before the night is out," she moaned into his ear, but loud enough for Adalia to hear.

The guy coughed, nodded and hurried off like a good little minion. He positioned himself at the bar and raised two fingers, then tapped his feet, bobbed his head and stared back at Michelle.

"Wonderful to see you again, Ms. Montclair," Michelle said, her tone belying her true feelings.

"You, too." Adalia's reply was calm, and she drank more champagne to dull the residual nerves from being on this damn date in the first place.

"Are you enjoying Trent's company?" Michelle licked her red lipstick and clicked her tongue.

"I sure am," Adalia said with a sun-bright smile. "We get on really well."

"Yeah, I noticed," Van Heerden said then glanced at her date and back to Adalia. A few of the other diners looked over at them; several of the women frowned at the sight of the model-like Michelle positioned close enough for their husband's to touch.

"Can I help you with something else? You delivered your message and interrupted our evening successfully, as I'm sure was your goal, but you're just standing there." Adalia lowered her voice, and traced a line on the tablecloth to signify her innocence. "I mean, no offense or anything, but you look kind of silly just hovering around here."

Michelle slid into the wooden-backed chair that Trent had vacated and propped her elbows on the table. "That's cute. Is that all you've got?"

"Oh, I'm sure you can ask Trent what I've got." Adalia spat it out and didn't allow herself to regret it. Van Heerden needed to be put in her place. "I admire your work ethic, coming all the way down here to give Trent that message, but there's such a thing as work appropriate attire. And that," Adalia paused, gesturing at the woman's cleavage, "is definitely not it."

"Oh, you like this?" Michelle leaned back and ran her fingers over the slopes of her breasts. "I'm sure Trent does, too."

"I'm sure I don't know why you're still sitting at this table."

"To deliver a message."

Adalia sighed at her stupidity and made it obvious. "You did that already."

"No, a different one. It's for you, but I guess you could call it more of a warning than a message."

"I'm all ears." She pushed back in her chair and cocked her head to one side, waiting for Ms. Bitch to lay it on thick. What would it be this time? An ultimatum? A death threat?

"Stay away from Trent Dawson."

"I've heard this all before."

"He's mine, do you understand me? I'll do whatever it takes to get you out of the way and out of his life." Michelle rammed her long nail into the table cloth to accentuate her point. "Whatever it takes."

"Including breaking your fake ass nails off? I'm terrified, girlie, but I've got bigger problems than your ego." Adalia waited a few seconds. This was the moment of truth for her... defending her feelings for Trent meant that she was all in. He was the one she wanted.

Michelle scraped back in her chair but Adalia reached out and gripped her arm.

The assistant stopped and raised both of her penciled eyebrows. "Let go of me."

"Here's my warning to you, chick. I don't ever back down, so if it's a fight you want, it's a fight you'll get. Though, it's pretty clear to me that Trent has already made his choice." She tossed the assistant's arm away and dropped her shoulders, relaxing her entire body.

Michelle tensed up and stood. "Watch your back."

"That's what I've got you for."

Adalia wasn't going to give up Trent – she'd fallen too hard and too fast for that. She wanted to know him better, to see him for who he really was, rather than the mystery of his character.

Trent appeared in the doorway and strolled over to them with a broad smile, though he paused to shake his head at Michelle and wave her off.

"Is it good news, sir?"

"I'll talk to you at work on Monday," he replied, settling into his seat and lifting his drink.

"Are you sure?" Michelle tried to entice him again, jiggling on the spot in mock excitement, but Trent didn't reply. His gaze was fixed on Adalia.

"I'm sorry for the interruption," he said.

"It's no problem, really, I understand about work."

"That's great," he replied, then looked for their waiter. "You still hungry?"

Michelle hovered nearby, waiting for another dismissal or an opportunity to interrupt.

"Well," Adalia said, running her forefinger down the length of his forearm and to the tip of his thumb, "I was thinking we could do that after."

"After." He smirked. "Let's settle the bill and get out of here."

Trent pulled back her chair and she escorted him to the maître d' with a Cheshire-cat smile.

She made sure to shoot it back over her shoulder at Van Heerden, who stood glaring after them with her date tugging at her arm.

Trent Dawson was her man now.

Chapter Sixteen

"So, this is what a billionaire's house looks like." Adalia stood in the massive entrance hall with its marble floors, wearing a sheepish grin.

"Let's go through to the living room and have a drink. Calm the nerves," he replied and she chuckled, the mirth chiming beneath the vaulted ceiling.

A flight of stairs led up to a second floor, curving inward to create an alarming geometric effect, but he led her off the main hall and into a wood-paneled living room with a plush red wall-to-wall carpet.

He gestured to the leather couch and she lowered herself onto it. "This place is beautiful."

"Thanks, I had an interior decorator come in to get it done, but I provided him with a general idea."

"You must be so relaxed when you get home from work. This place is a palace."

"Yeah, I guess," he said and shrugged.

This was her solid small talk, because of that growing desire to consume him.

The rooms were artfully decorated, but sparse, as if he didn't have time for frivolities. That suited what she knew of him pretty darn well.

Trent opened up a mini-bar in the wall and brought out a bottle of Cognac and two glasses. He filled them with ice from a dispenser then came over to join her. He poured the liquid into the tumbler and handed it to her, but she swilled it around without drinking.

There was too much heat in the room. She could hardly breathe, let alone drink alcohol.

"I'm glad I have you here," he muttered, swilling the Cognac in the glass, but also not drinking it. She stared at his lips, willing them to move again, to say her name.

"I'm glad to be here." It was the absolute truth and it freed her from the angst she'd carried around about this man since they'd met. "I know I resisted this, but I really am glad we got to talk tonight."

He took the glass from her and placed it on his coffee table, following with his own.

"What are you doing?'

"What we should have done a long time ago." He grasped the back of her head, running his hand up into her hair, and drew her toward him.

"Oh God," she whispered. This was it. She'd fantasized about this moment since he'd had her on her couch in her crummy apartment.

"Adalia," he groaned and she reacted instantly, pressing her lips to his.

He parted them and tasted her, searching for more. She gave it all, breathing into him, moaning for more than just a taste this time.

Trent was alive for her, grasping at the back of her dress. He pulled the zipper down and she stood quickly then struggled out of it. He ripped his own shirt off and unbuckled his pants. Their need for each other was over the top.

There was no time to waste.

"I have to have you," she muttered.

"Beg for it."

"Please, Trent, I need you." She slipped out of her sodden panties, turned and bent over so he could see everything. She was laid bare for him, ready for the taking.

"Fuck," he growled, "Adalia, baby, you're gorgeous."

"Take me." She wiggled her ass at him, teasing as best she could, though she couldn't articulate just how much her desire had grown. She was at peak capacity.

His hands gripped her hips, but he didn't enter her yet. He undid her bra instead and released her breasts, then reached around and played with them, caressing. He pinched her nipples and she groaned.

Then he lowered his mouth to her back and kissed a line of heat up to her shoulder.

"Not like this."

Disappointment threatened to overwhelm her. "What?"

"Follow me," Trent answered, then took her by the hand and led her out of the room. His erection was enormous, and they were both naked, but there wasn't a chance of interference.

He took her up those winding stairs, glancing back every few moments and showing her his intent with a soulful expression. There was so much more than lust there.

They entered his bedroom and she gasped. White Egyptian cotton sheets, throw pillows in black satin, and a tranquil aesthetic.

"Lie down."

She followed his orders and positioned herself on the king-sized bed. He crawled up it, and over her body, kissing her legs, then the insides of her thighs. Trent parted her legs, ran a finger between her lips.

He placed his mouth over her clit and sucked on it, kissing and slurping, and she slammed both her arms upward and gripped at the pillows.

She moaned and circled her hips. He went with the motion, giving small moans of satisfaction. "You taste so good," he said, and she gripped the top of his head, hanging on for dear life. "I've wanted to do this since we first met."

He broke away and inserted two fingers inside her, and she arched her back. He went slow then massaged her G-spot, caressing her so intimately that she shattered to pieces under his touch.

"You're going to come for me," he said, and she gasped, nodding frantically and slapping the bedspread. She gripped it and pulled hard, searching for leverage.

Trent lowered his mouth to her folds and explored, using his tongue to devour her.

"I'm so close," she groaned.

"Good. Come for me."

The command sent her over the edge and waves of pleasure shuddered through her. She raised her hips and pressed herself into his mouth.

"Oh yes," he grunted.

She gasped his name over and over again.

Her mind blacked out. There was only them and the overwhelming sense of bliss.

Adalia's ass hit the bed and she let out a final moan. "That was unbelievable."

"We're not done yet," he said, getting onto his knees between her legs. He parted them even more, then lowered himself on top of her and kissed her forehead, her cheeks, her nose and finally her mouth.

She could taste herself on him and it drove her wild all over again.

"I need you." Adalia wrapped her legs around his waist and tried to tease his dick inside her, but he evaded her.

"I know," he chuckled, "and I need you."

"Give it to me." She pouted like a spoiled brat and his mirth doubled.

"How bad do you want it, baby?" The sentence came out soft and her mouth went dry. There was so much meaning in it.

Trent kissed her again, increasing the pressure of his lips.
"So bad."

"How bad?"

"More than anything."

He plunged into her, immersing himself in her velvet warmth and she cried out and gripped his back. Acute pain and pleasure mingled into a harmony and she was lost.

He went slow and deep, and they moved together, creating a rhythm that matched the beat of her heart. She was at ease with him, but aroused past the point of speech.

Adalia stared up at him above her, moving and never shifting his gaze from hers.

They were one.

"Adalia," he murmured, then buried his face in her neck, kissing and nibbling her skin.

She gripped the back of his neck. "Come for me," she whispered, and he growled.

His thrusts sped up and he pounded into her, probing for his orgasm. Adalia clung to him, gasping, and the beginnings of another orgasm washed over her.

"Oh God, I'm coming," she moaned.

"Adalia," he cried and rammed himself into the beginnings of his own orgasm.

They climaxed together, gripping each other tight. They melted and became one, dissolving past the normal spectrum of physical pleasure.

This was deeper, more meaningful.

She knew his soul.

"I love you," he whispered.

Chapter Seventeen

Adalia cracked open an eyelid the next morning, but the room was plunged in darkness. The thick curtains in Trent's room didn't let in a single ray of light.

She rolled over and checked the alarm clock beside his bed. It was already 9am. She should be at work, but it was a Friday and no one would come in anyway. Adalia sat up and rubbed the sleep from her eyes.

Trent lay beside her, snoring slightly, his ripped abs visible even underneath the sheet.

What a delicious treat. She'd had the most amazing night with him – living, feeling, breathing.

Riiiiiing.

Her phone sounded in the bedroom and she jumped up. She hurried over to her bag and whipped it out, then squinted at the screen. She didn't recognize the number, and that was never good.

Adalia padded out of the room, glancing left and right in case Trent had a maid or the like. She hadn't bothered throwing a shirt on, let alone slipping into her dress – that was still downstairs with his pants.

"Hello?" she answered and strolled to the balustrade, then leaned on it.

"Is this Ms. Adalia Montclair?"

"Yes, this is she." She gripped the metal banister with one hand and steeled herself.

"Ms. Montclair, I'm calling from the bank with regards to your overdue loan repayments." It was a woman this time, and she sounded as cold as the air in the hall.

"How can I help you?"

"Unfortunately, I'm calling to inform you that you've missed your deadline for repayment."

What could she say to that?

"If you give me just another month I can come up with the money, I swear it." Adalia gritted her teeth at the thought of asking Trent, but maybe that was the only way. She could pay him back with interest once she had the money.

She half-turned to walk back to the bedroom then halted.

"That won't be possible, Ms. Montclair."

"To whom am I speaking?"

"This is Mrs. Laurent. Regrettably –"

Adalia popped her hip and placed her fist on it. "Hold on just one moment, Mrs. Laurent, and hear me out, okay?"

"Ms. Montclair –"

"Please, hasn't anyone ever given you a chance before? Just let me say what I have to say and after that you can do what you see fit. All right?"

There was a long silence on the other end of the line as the woman mulled it over.

A door slammed somewhere in the mansion, and Adalia covered her breasts with one arm and snuck down the hall, searching for privacy.

"Very well," the bank woman replied.

Adalia opened a door and peered into the room beyond. A bath and toilet stared back at her, so she flicked the light switch and went in then shut the door behind her.

"I've been through a tough time with the bakery, I spent all the money the bank loaned me on buying equipment, setting up the front end of the bakery and hiring help," she said, ticking the points off on her fingers.

"All right, but what you did with the money is truly your prerogative and business." Mrs. Laurent put in and Adalia coughed over her words.

"You need the full picture to understand what I'm about to say," she answered, and the woman went silent. Maybe this one was less of a Kraken than the last old fart who'd called her.

"Ms. Montclair, it's June 23rd, it's far past your date for repayment and the bank has no choice but –"

"You haven't let me finish," Adalia said, forcing herself to speak slowly and clearly. If she snapped, she'd lose the audience immediately.

She glared at the potted plant in the corner, waggling its fronds under the extractor fan. She grimaced at the extra noise in the room, but didn't turn off the light.

"Go ahead," said the banker, but her tone spoke volumes as to how pointless Adalia's endeavor was. She'd never listen, but she had to try and make her see sense.

"To bring in more money and more customers, I need to market the business, but I haven't been able to do that, because, like I said, I used the loan to create it in the first place."

"Unfortunately, Ms. Montclair, that expense is something you should have included in the business plan you presented to the bank when applying for your loan."

"Oh, I know, and that was my mistake. I'm not accusing the bank of anything, I'm just explaining my situation here."

The woman sighed. "Ms. Montclair, I understand that you need more money, but the bank can't provide it to you given your current credit record."

The light overhead was a dull yellow, but she didn't bother turning the knob beneath the switch to brighten the room.

"I don't need you to provide me with the money. I have an investor who could help me pay off the twenty-thousand dollars I owe now and help me set up the marketing aspect further. I just need a few days, not even a week, to organize it." Adalia crossed her fingers, thumbs, toes and legs.

Surely the woman would see that she was serious?

"Ms. Montclair, I appreciate you explaining your situation to me and I empathize with you, but it is June 23rd and your loan repayment was due on the 15th."

"I'm well aware of that, trust me, but if you could just…"

Mrs. Laurent cleared her throat this time and Adalia snapped her mouth shut.

"Because of your inability to fulfill your financial obligation to the bank, I am calling to inform you that your assets will be liquidated."

Adalia's heart sank into the pit of her stomach. She'd known it would happen eventually, but not now, not like this. There had to be something she could do! This was her dream, what she'd fantasized about doing as a little girl.

"Please, give me a chance to contact my investor and have them pay you the money within the next few days. Surely you can cut me a break here." Adalia sat on the edge of the bath and gripped it hard. It was icy cold, but she didn't flinch away.

Her mind was focused on the bakery, on making this uppity bank chick realize that this was it for her. This was her life.

"I'm sorry, Ms. Montclair."

"No, you're not," she snapped, finally erupting under the pressure of Mrs. Laurent's resolve to ignore her pleas. "You're not sorry at all. You won't even give me a few days to gather my affairs so I can make this right."

"Ms. Montclair, you've been provided with ample opportunities to make your repayments and to organize a repayment scheme. You took neither of these opportunities, and unfortunately, the onus for this failure is not on the bank." Her implication was clear.

Adalia was the failure in this. She had let it slip right out of her fingers by her inability to bring in enough money to repay these bastards.

Nausea battered against the lining of her stomach and she gripped at herself.

"Don't you see? Don't you understand? The bakery is all that I have, it's my world. If you take that away I'll have nothing left."

"Good day, Ms. Montclair." The line went dead. Adalia was greeted with the empty dial tone, which drove home the hard point that her business was gone.

Without it, she'd be unable to live in her apartment, to afford food, water, electricity... *anything*. She was officially at breaking point.

Her next move was crucial.

Adalia buried her pride deep and stood up, clutching the phone in her right hand. She'd have to ask Trent for help. There wasn't any other option.

Chapter Eighteen

"Trent?" Adalia called his name softly to wake him up then let herself into his bedroom.

But it wasn't dark anymore, and he wasn't in the bed. Instead, a tanned housekeeper stood over it, pulling the sheets into place.

"Oh my God," Adalia whispered and tried to back out of the room, covering her bits and pieces, but there were far too many curves to accommodate for.

The housekeeper looked up and shrieked, then clapped her hand to her mouth to shut out the sound. "*Lo siento*," she whispered past her fingers.

"That's all right, don't worry." Adalia gripped the phone and used it to cover one nipple, then blocked her privates with her other hand. Her clothes were downstairs and the maid surely didn't know how to avert her gaze. "Could you hand me a towel from the bathroom?"

The maid didn't move.

"Or a blanket off the bed? Pillow? Anything? No?"

Adalia crept sideways toward the dresser, shifted it open and rooted around inside it for a shirt.

The housekeeping lady stiffened and frowned, and Adalia shot her a quick look of disdain. Like she would steal from the man she'd slept with. *Bitch, please.*

Adalia brought out a shirt, some baseball team's logo printed across the front of it, and slipped it over her head. Luckily, Trent was bigger and taller than she was; the bottom covered the tops of her thighs.

The other woman relaxed slightly, now that she was covered up.

"I didn't realize anyone was in here," she said, and the maid bobbed her head, though her glare said she hadn't understood a word. "Where's Trent?"

"*No entiendo Ingles*," the housekeeper said, raising her palms.

Didn't the woman understand her boss' name?

"Trent Dawson?" she asked again, searching the room for a picture of him, but there were none. Not even a graduation photo or anything. "He's the owner of this house? Your boss, Trent."

The maid gaped at her, mouth flapping open and closed. She bent and picked up a feather duster, then held it out as if it were a shield.

"You really have no English at all?"

"*No entiendo Ingles.*" The woman blinked and twirled the duster slowly, then shook her head in total miscomprehension. Trying to get through to her would take weeks.

"That's all right. Thanks, I'll wait here." Adalia smiled but the maid shook her head, expression blank. "I will wait," she said, signaling and then pointing to the floor. "Here."

The maid fluffed her short cropped curly hair then shuffled toward the door without another word. The bed was made at least, but the housekeeper seemed unwilling to stay a moment longer. Thank God.

She let herself out, murmuring apologies in Spanish. "*Lo siento, lo siento,*" she said and Adalia finally found the humor in the situation and burst out laughing. The woman jumped and hurried out faster, and she shut the door behind her.

What a morning. As if things could get any more complicated.

Adalia strolled to the bed and sat down on Trent's side, then placed her phone next to his on the bedside table. The bank situation was disastrous, but it might not be irreconcilable.

She settled onto the duvet cover with a beleaguered sigh, staring directly at the wall of windows that looked out onto the city. Her bakery was out in that mess. Cars sped through the streets, between high rises and low buildings, hooting and letting off exhaust fumes.

There were apartment blocks, malls, and banks, everything a big city needed. Buildings galore and hers was somewhere in the middle of them. Ignored, lost to customers.

Adalia stood and opened the smallest window to the right, letting in a gust of fresh air. She closed her eyes and let it blow away her fear and pain. It didn't work and the cloying scent of city smog made her eyes water.

She closed it again and backed off, then sat back down on the bed, smoothing the sheets to soothe her mind. The texture was quality personified.

The world flowed forward, ceaseless, and it didn't matter what she wanted or who she was. Nobody cared about her problems except for her, and that was true of everyone. If she couldn't deal with it, too bad. There was no one else to deal with it for her.

And that suited her fine on most days. In most years, even, it was just the sore fact that this was out of her control, which hit home.

She didn't have the money and she couldn't save her dream without lowering herself and asking for help. Begging for it really.

Where was he?

She bounced around and crossed her knees.

Beep, beep.

The message tone on her phone went off, and she swept it up off the bedside table and scrolled through to her messages. Who could this be? The last thing she needed was DeShawn's interference.

I can't wait to see you.

She frowned and rolled her eyes, then glanced at the name on top of the screen. Her heart froze. Michelle Van Heerden stared back at her, and she blinked several times. Michelle couldn't wait to see her?

This had to be some kind of sick joke.

Adalia exited the message and scanned her inbox, but she didn't recognize any of the names except for the assistant's. This wasn't her phone.

She glanced at the bedside table and gasped. It was Trent's phone.

Adalia couldn't help herself.

She opened up another of Michelle's messages and her heart sank through her chest, through her diaphragm and into her stomach, a lead weight of despair.

I'm going to suck your cock so hard, you'll go cross-eyed, baby. Can't wait to see the look on your face when I walk into the office today.

Adalia thumbed the screen of the smartphone and opened up another.

You look so good in that suit I just wanna rip it right off your hot bod.

And another.

Wanna fuck you so hard. Just get on top and ride you until you can't take it anymore. Don't you want that, too? Treat you so good, baby, all night long.

Adalia gripped the phone and breathed through her mouth. This couldn't be true, he couldn't have lied to her about this all along.

She slammed the phone back on the bedside table and picked up her own.

She'd been such a fool. He'd tricked her into believing this was true after all her doubts and she'd still gone with it.

Two dreams shattered in the span of a day. She'd never ask for his help now, she'd sooner hit him as look at him, let alone talk to that bastard. Sobs racked her body and her vision blurred with tears.

She'd fallen for the creep. She'd actually allowed him into her heart, in spite of everything.

Adalia rose and looked down at the T-shirt, Trent's shirt, then ripped it over her head and threw it on the bed.

She was naked, and she had nothing but her handbag with her. She lifted if off the floor – Trent had fetched it for her the night before, in case she got an important call – and slung it over her bare shoulder.

Then she ripped his bedroom door open and marched out into the hallway.

"Trent!" she yelled at the top of her lungs and the cleaning lady poked her head out of the bathroom nearby, started and disappeared again. "Trent Dawson, where are you?"

Adalia stormed down that spiral staircase, as naked as she'd been going up it, but with her heart so broken she wasn't sure if it would beat for much longer.

She hurt so much, she was sure she'd collapse.

But that just wasn't her style.

Chapter Nineteen

Adalia charged down the stairs, naked feet slapping on the marble. She didn't care about the cold, or her naked body wobbling around for anyone to see.

"Trent!" she yelled louder this time, and heard a noise from the living room.

She walked in then stopped dead. Trent was there all right, but he wasn't alone. An old man in a suit and lurid tie, with a pair of specs perched atop his bald head sat with him, staring at her as if she'd lost her mind.

Maybe she had.

"Adalia," Trent said, coloring blood red. "What the hell are you doing?"

She searched the room for her dress and found it lying folded neatly atop the bar. She dumped her bag on the floor, pulled it on and half-zipped it up without his help. He tried to do the rest, but she smacked him away.

The old dude rose from the sofa with a warm smile. "I'm Withnail Harrington," he said in a heavy British accent, and extended his pale wrinkled hand. "It's a pleasure to make your acquaintance."

"Yeah, whatever," she snapped back and ignored his friendly gesture. She wasn't a rude person, but her anger had destroyed the need for niceties.

"Adalia," Trent growled, "greet my guest properly." He wore a loose shirt and slacks, and he'd obviously not showered yet. This guy was probably the tycoon he'd phoned the night before.

So what!

"I can't believe you." The rage bubbled over into a low shriek.

Withnail Harrington faltered, taking several steps backward. "I could come back another time, Mr. Dawson, if you have more pressing matters to attend to."

Trent studied her expression. "No, that's fine, Mr. Harrington, please stay and make yourself comfortable. It's clear that Adalia wants to make a scene, so let's let her have one."

"I really think I should go." The old man edged further away.

"Actually, it's not that I can't believe you, I just can't believe I was stupid enough to allow this to happen." Adalia's eyes burned with hatred, and she stared at the man she'd fallen for, the goddamn billionaire player, so hard that strain set in at her temples. She didn't bother massage the pressure away… it fueled her fury at him.

"I have no idea what you're talking about."

Harrington hovered in the doorway, torn between leaving and fetching a bowl of popcorn, apparently. He wore a mixed expression of horror and fascination like a wrinkly mask.

"I found the messages, Trent. I know you're sleeping with her."

"That's my cue," Harrington said, then waved to them both. "I'll call you sometime, Trent. Let me know when you've got a minute." Then he disappeared, whisking off into the distance.

"You might have lost me the deal of a lifetime right now." Trent clapped once.

"I don't care."

"Of course you don't. You only care about yourself, Adalia Montclair," he spat, then kicked the coffee table in the first true expression of anger she'd ever seen from him.

"Stop deflecting, you bastard."

"You realize you chased off one of the most influential men in the world, and definitely one of the richest. If I lose this deal because of you, I'll –"

"You'll what, Trent? Cheat on me? I would be scared, but it looks like you've already done that. Man, I can't believe I was so stupid to trust you." She yelled the last sentence.

"Seriously, have you gone mad? What the fuck are you talking about?" Trent strolled to the bar and brought out a bottle of water. He opened it and tossed some back, a fine line of fluid trickled out of the corner of his mouth and down his tan neck.

"I know about Michelle, Trent. I saw all the messages on your phone."

"And you assume that I'm cheating on you? God, we have to be dating before you can even assume that."

"We're not dating," Adalia said in a monotone then cracked out laughing. "Of course we're not. You wouldn't date the likes of me. You prefer tight little Valley girls with minimal brains and maximum cleavage."

"You need to calm down. You're jumping to conclusions."

But she was on a roll, and she wouldn't be placated.

"I should've known, but I went against my instincts." She paced back and forth in front of him, barefoot, but at least her body was concealed. "Typical Adalia luck… the day I find out that the bank is liquidating my bakery is the day I discover your fucking infidelity."

"You lost the bakery?" Trent's brow furrowed, but he didn't move toward her. And it was better that way – she was two seconds away from physically accosting him.

"You've humiliated me! No wonder that Michelle cow is insistent on getting you into bed. It's because she's already had you and knows that you're making a fool of me, too."

"I have never slept with Michelle Van Heerden. Not once in my fucking life, so can we move past that point and discuss the real issue here?"

Adalia stopped pacing, and leaned on the back of his couch, shaking her head and losing steam for a second.

"You can say what you want to me, Trent, but I know that it's all lies. You can't tell me the truth now, even after I've caught you. Sickening," she said. "I should've left without confronting you about this, but I couldn't bring myself to give you the satisfaction of an easy lay."

He smacked himself on the forehead and pointed at her. "You're starting to make me angry now. I'm gonna red line, Adalia. Don't make me fucking red line, you will regret it."

She hopped over the couch, as nimble as a ballerina, and charged up to him. She forced her face right up into his and growled, "What are you going to do, Trent? Hit me?"

"You're fucking crazy. You're forcing my hand, pushing me over the edge."

"Come on, big man, what are you going to do? You wanna beat on a woman? I've had worse in my life. I've had worse than you and worse than this embarrassment."

"Get out of my way." He turned and slammed his hand into the coffee table. There was a tremendous 'crack' and it split clean down the middle.

"What are you doing? You'll injure yourself."

"I don't care," he replied, and straightened. There was blood dripping from the hand he'd used and his knuckles were a mangled mess.

"I don't have time for this drama. I've lost my dream and you've humiliated me to the core. That's enough for one day." Adalia marched to the door, the back of her dress still flapping open, but she didn't bother trying to close it herself.

"Where are you going?" He glared at her, trembling with both hands balled into fists.

"Away. I can't go home… I'm going to lose it pretty soon. So, away, not that it's any of your business."

"You haven't given me a chance to explain."

She paused, swept up her handbag and shouldered it. "I don't need your explanations. This is over."

"I'll call you when you've cooled down," he replied, but Adalia shook her head. He just didn't get it, and he never would.

"Don't bother calling me ever again. I'm not interested."

"You can't give up this easily." His tone dripped with disappointment, but that made no difference. He didn't know what disappointment was. She did... finding out the man of her dreams was sleeping with someone else and had used her as a pawn for sex.

She laughed at herself.

"I'm not giving up. I'm just done."

"With what?"

Adalia turned back one last time and skewered his soul with a hateful gaze. "You."

Chapter Twenty

"Everything will be all right, my girl, this was meant to happen." Adalia's dad hugged her tight, and then helped her cart her bags over the threshold of his home.

"What do you mean, Dad?" Adalia tugged her bag in, but he lifted it for her and marched it through to her old room. "How will it be all right? I don't see it right now."

"Trust me. This is what was meant to happen."

"Why?"

"Everything in life happens for a reason," he said simply, as if it was the plainest fact in the world.

"And what's that?" She looked around the old room with its single bed and plain white dresser.

"The reason is to teach you a lesson. Life wants you to learn something from this and it's up to you to take that lesson and run with it. Adapt, rethink, stand up fighting."

"That's easier said than done."

"That's life, girl." He patted her on the shoulder, and she remained tense. "Life is supposed to kick you down from time to time, just to make sure you know your place."

"What's my place, Dad? Is this it? Is my place to be a failure before I even hit thirty?"

He sighed and turned her by the shoulders to face him. "My girl, your place is where you know it is, in here," he said, pointing to her heart, "not in here," he continued, gesturing to her forehead. "You've got to reconcile what you want and what you can do to get it. If you don't, you'll end up back here every time things go wrong."

She stared at him, jaw hanging open slightly. He didn't usually speak all that much.

"I'll leave you to get settled in. Dinner at six." Then he shuffled out and closed the door behind him.

Adalia's entire body drooped.

Here she was in her old house, a place she'd never thought she'd return to, but what choice did she have? It was this or live on the streets.

She'd failed at everything, but the streets were still beyond her. She wanted to believe there was a manner of salvaging this, but she didn't envision an answer. Her reality had turned dark, and she waded through the fog of depression.

Adalia sat down on her old creaking bed and fingered the hole in her floral bedspread. She'd planned the bakery in this room, dreamed up her bright future and been so convinced she could do anything if she put her mind to it.

That was a load of bullshit if she'd ever heard it.

There was no hope left.

Riiiiiiing.

She let out a low groan. She'd had about twenty missed calls from Trent in the past few days and hadn't returned any of them.

Adalia drew out her phone and pressed her lips together. Sure enough, Trent's name flashed on the screen, lighting up her memories of him.

Her thumb hovered over the red phone icon. She shifted it to the green.

"Yes?"

"Finally," he said, and that deep voice sent shivers down her spine, soon replaced by the color of anger racing up her throat.

"What do you want, Trent? I told you not to contact me again."

"I have news I think you might find quite pleasing. In fact, I'm sure of it." He was totally at ease and it made her angrier. How was it that he thought everything was fine when it clearly wasn't?

"You've got about five seconds before I hang up the phone."

"Don't give me an ultimatum. I'm doing you a favor right now."

"I don't need your fucking favors," she barked, and pulled the phone away to hang up.

"I can help you get the bakery back."

Adalia froze and stared at the screen, with Trent's image displayed. The bakery back?

"Adalia? Are you there?"

"Yeah, I'm here," she replied, placing the phone back on her ear and lying down on the bed with a squeak.

"What was that?"

"None of your damn business."

"You're about as friendly as a bear with a hedgehog up its ass." Trent was clearly losing patience, but she couldn't help pushing him – it was justified after what he'd done.

"That's what happens when you have sex with a bimbo, I guess."

"You're still on that? You never gave me a chance to explain, but if that's the way you want to play this then fine."

"Play this? The only person who's playing here is you. I was serious… I put myself on the line. I even fell into bed with you."

"I meant everything I said."

"To who? Me or Michelle?" Adalia grunted the question, but the answer would never be satisfactory. He was a liar, and she'd never believe him. Never!

"We'll get to that another time. There are more important issues at hand."

"Spit it out." She stretched her arm upward and gripped the back of the bed, then closed her eyes, picturing she was back in her own tiny apartment, lying on the couch. A month ago she'd had it all.

"I bought your bakery on auction from the bank."

Adalia's insides turned to molten lava. Her eyes snapped open. "Pardon?"

"I bought your bakery, and I want you to run it. I'll give you the money you need for marketing, to hire help, anything you want, with no strings attached. I'll be your silent partner, consider it an investment in who you are as a person."

Adalia sat bolt upright, then lurched off the bed with a telling creak.

"What do you say?"

"I say you're an interfering asshole."

"What?" Trent shouted then lowered his voice. "Adalia, do you realize what I'm offering you here?"

She stormed to her bedroom window and pulled it up, then stared out at the streets below. There was a guy with low-slung jeans dealing pot on the corner. Across from that there was a group of kids playing jump rope near a bright red fire hydrant.

It was a hood scene out of a movie, for God's sake, and she wanted nothing more than to escape before crime or danger swallowed her whole.

"Adalia?"

"You're offering me a handout not a hand up. I'm not interested."

He clicked his teeth. "I didn't do this to make you feel small, only to give you the big break you deserve."

"No, you did it because you feel guilty about what you did with Van Heerden, and I have no interest in your guilt money. I can't believe you would interfere in my life like this. I can't believe you think this is justified."

A group of guys came around the corner, chatting. They stopped and stared at the pot dealer. Uh oh, trouble brewing. Maybe it was a turf war. The kids had noticed, too – they cleared off, disappearing into a block of flats across the road.

Her dad's tiny lawn was well-groomed, but they trampled over it in their haste to get away.

"Adalia, this is your last chance. Either you take this offer or I turn that place into something else. I've got plenty of uses for a building like that." The threat fell on deaf ears. She didn't want his help or his money – she'd been right not to trust him and she wouldn't start again now.

Once bitten and all that crap.

The pot dealer flicked his jacket back to reveal a pistol in the belt of his jeans.

The men across from him yelled something.

"Last chance."

"Goodbye, Trent."

Shots fired and screams rang out. Adalia hung up the phone, turned and walked back to her bed. There was a swift knock at the door and her father entered.

"I called the cops. Just wanted to check you were all right."

"I'm fine," she lied.

Chapter Twenty-One

Adalia sat on the front porch in the dark and stared up at the stars. The night sky was free of clouds, and the streetlamp outside her dad's house had shorted, so she could see it all.

There was Orion's Belt and the moon, the Southern Cross and Scorpio.

Her brother, Michael, had a strong interest in the stars and had lectured her on the constellations for hours on end. As a result, she knew a whole bunch of stuff about the stars she didn't particularly care for, but it came in handy on a night like this.

The commotion of the past week was over, the cops had cleared off the culprits and no one had died, by some small miracle.

A man yelled in an apartment across the road, and the sharp crack of glass breaking echoed across the street, but she didn't get up and go inside. That kind of thing was normal and she needed this.

The bakery was gone and she'd rejected Trent, but it was for the best.

She'd find some course of action, but not right then. She needed a few days, weeks, months to recuperate after this shit. He'd nearly destroyed her.

She'd nearly destroyed herself with her failures.

"You coming in, girl?" Her father stood behind her, casting a shadow on the pavement in front of her. A daddy-shaped shadow. She flashed back to her childhood, to playing on the street and laughing with her brother.

It'd seemed so simple back then. Play, go to school, stay out of trouble, miss Momma. And now it was none of those things except for the last one when she let it get to her.

"No, I think I'll stay out a while longer."

"All right, but I'm going to bed. You be safe out here," he said, and the shadow's overgrown head swiveled left and right, checking the street.

"Thanks, Dad, I'll be okay."

He turned and disappeared into the house, but left the front door open, just in case.

Adalia smiled in spite of the ache in the center of her chest. At least she had her dad and her brother if he ever deigned to visit again. She didn't blame him for staying away – they'd never felt they belonged in the hood.

A figure appeared at the end of the street and strolled up it in a familiar gait. She froze and stared, then shook her head. The man stopped at the end of the pathway and stared up at her.

"What do you want?" she asked without anger, more with interest.

"I heard what happened, baby," DeShawn said. "I wanted to check you was all right, after that bakery thing didn't work out."

"Way to bring it to the forefront, DeShawn," she replied, giving him a sarcastic thumbs up.

"Whatcha mean?"

"Nothing," she said then stared at the three stars of Orion's Belt. He sidled up the pathway and sat down on the porch beside her, hiking up his jeans and balancing both forearms on his knees.

"I miss you, girl," he said then brushed her earlobe with his forefinger. There were no chills of desire from that action, but there weren't shivers of revulsion either.

"Do you know what that is?" she asked, pointing up at the sky, and he grunted his confusion. "I thought so."

"That a satellite or somethin'?"

"That's Orion's Belt. Those three stars that are kind of in a weird row. They're called Orion's Belt, and they're part of the constellation of Orion."

"Aight," he replied, but he didn't ask any question about the constellation.

She told him anyway. "Did you know that the Pyramids of Giza are perfectly aligned with Orion's Belt?"

"No shit," he said, and a hint of awe entered his tone. It satisfied her that she'd gotten through to him in some small way, and made him think further than the next bong, a feat she'd been unable to accomplish throughout the duration of their relationship.

"Yeah, no shit. That's symmetry. Dreams aligned with reality, working in perfect harmony to create something amazing, something no one will ever forget."

"So," he said, then squeezed her thigh, "maybes some day you find your Orion's Belt, Dalie." Another pet name he'd used for her during their time together. Agony sprouted in her chest and took such strong root that she lost her breath.

She buckled over and hugged her knees, and DeShawn stroked her back with care.

"You okay, baby?"

"No," she murmured, overcome by the need to scream or cry. She didn't let it out… she wouldn't show him that weakness, no matter how much it hurt her to keep it all inside.

"I wanna help you."

"You can't help me, DeShawn, you can't even help yourself."

"What that mean?" He stopped stroking and sniffed. She straightened slowly, and the pressure around her heart loosened incrementally.

"Have you quit smoking weed?" she asked outright because she was past the point of being his sweetheart, his soft girl.

DeShawn flinched and didn't answer the question, which was answer enough for her.

"I think you should go, DeShawn. Thanks for stopping by and trying to be nice, but I don't need anything but alone time, right now."

"You still messing around with that white guy?"

Adalia's pain redoubled and her back curved under the weight of it. "No," she murmured.

He nodded and pouted his lips. "Thought so. That kinda guy ain't for you, baby."

"Why's that?"

DeShawn shrugged, opened his mouth then closed it and grinned. "He just ain't, take my word for it, girl."

"I can't take your word for anything. I can't trust you." Or anyone else.

"Yeah, you can." DeShawn moved closer, until their hips touched, and slipped his arm around her waist. "I want you back, Dalie, I can't live wit'out you."

Adalia's heart pined for affection, but this guy wasn't it. He wouldn't give her what she needed, and he deserved better than to be led on by her. It wouldn't be fair to him or her.

"No, DeShawn, I don't want to be with you or anyone, right now." She tried to move away but he held her tight and she couldn't squirm away. She didn't have the energy for a fight either. "Let me go, DeShawn. We can talk about this another time, but not tonight, okay? I can't handle it right now."

"Why not?" He still didn't move off.

"Because my daughter told you so." Her dad strolled onto the porch and glared at DeShawn. "You want to start something you can't finish again, boy? I suggest you get off my porch and away from my house before I call the damn cops."

DeShawn hopped up and moseyed down the stairs trying to look cool. He raised his hand but didn't look back. "I'll call you, baby."

Adalia didn't have the strength to tell him not to. She didn't care about him or anything else, only about going inside, flopping down on her old bed and sleeping the pain away.

"Are you all right, my girl?" Her father offered her a hand, and she took it then rose to her feet.

"I don't know anymore, Daddy," she said, then burst into tears. He wrapped his arms around her and made the cooing noises he'd used the night her mother had died.

"Everything will be fine, baby girl. In the end, everything will be fine."

Adalia sniffed and he walked her inside and to her bedroom.

"How do you know that, Dad?"

"I just do."

He closed the door and let her get some rest, but she tossed and turned late into the night, Trent's gorgeous face swimming in front of her eyes.

A vision of pain.

Chapter Twenty-Two

Adalia pushed the Sunday night roast beef around on her plate, but didn't spear it and pop it into her mouth. She and her father had made the gravy together, but she couldn't recall much of the process. Seconds and minutes melded into one another, became a blur of wasted time.

"Adalia?"

"Pardon?" She snapped her attention off the plate and to her father's face. "What's wrong?"

"That's exactly what I asked you, five times. Are you all right?"

"Not really," she replied, dropping her fork. She massaged her eyes with the heels of her palms, but there weren't tears to chase away. She was fresh out of tears. They'd been replaced by constant numbness.

"This isn't about the bakery," he observed, scratching at his chin. "I've seen you disappointed before, but not like this."

"It's complicated, Dad," she replied, but didn't go into more detail. The less he knew about Trent Dawson, the better. He'd probably freak out at her if he found out she had feelings for him.

"Is this about the billionaire?"

"When did you become a mind reader?" She pushed her plate away, totally out of reach and he raised an eyebrow at her. "Yes, Dad, it's about him."

"Break it down for me. What's happened?"

Adalia glanced out the front window of the living room to the street outside. There were no cars, and the sunset had cast an orange glow over the neighborhood. Children's laughter rang out and the soft thump of music.

It wasn't unpleasant, but the familiarity gave her the chills.

"I fell in love with him."

"I thought so, but what's the problem? What happened between you two that's got you moping around here like your cat died?"

She snorted a laugh and he wriggled his eyebrows in the cheeky way he'd done when they were kids. It'd always gotten a laugh out of them and relieved the tension when there was too much.

Too much homework and the eyebrows wriggled. Too few friends, and they wriggled again.

"It's a long story, Dad."

"I've got time," he replied, spreading his arms wide and pushing his plate away too, though it was empty of food.

"He played me. I thought he loved me, or felt the way I did, but it turns out he was sleeping with his assistant all along. What a damn cliché."

"You actually saw them together?"

"Well, no," she said, scratching at her forehead, "but there were some nasty messages on his phone."

"Why were you snooping through his phone?" he asked, eyebrows drawn down instead of wriggling in amusement.

"It was an accident," she replied.

"If you say so."

"Are my ears deceiving me? Are you actually taking his side?" Adalia poked her chin forward and glared at him.

"I've never been one to take sides, and I sure can't make a judgment just on what you're telling me, but sounds to me like you jumped to conclusions."

"He didn't even deny –" She cut herself off. Yeah, he had denied it, but she hadn't given him a chance to explain. Oh God, had she screwed this one up, too?

"What else is there to this? Just the assumed infidelity?"

"He bought my bakery."

"What?" Her father slapped his palms on the worn wood of the table, and launched himself forward. "He bought you out?"

"No, no, calm down," she replied, waving him back into his seat. "I lost the bakery to the bank. They took it away from me because I couldn't pay off my loan."

"What's that got to do with him?"

"He bought it and offered it to me. Said I could run it and he'd be a silent partner, no strings attached." Adalia shook her head and waited for her father to freak out again.

But he didn't. Instead, he sat back and folded his arms, frowning at her over the table.

"What?" she asked, glancing over her shoulder and into the kitchen, then back at him. "What is it?"

"You lost your mind?"

"People ask me that a lot lately."

"Maybe that's because you've lost your damn mind, girl," he said, raising his voice an iota.

"Uh, Dad? Why are you freaking out?"

"Because you're acting crazy, that's why. The man you're in love with offers to help you achieve your only dream, the dream you've been talking about for the past fifteen years, and you tell him no?"

"I had to, he just wanted to work with me so that we'd get close and he'd have a chance to get back with me." Adalia gripped the table, and the setting sun finally disappeared, leaving a purple haze in the room, a dusky effect that soothed them in lilacs.

"And so?"

"How can I trust him after what he did?"

"This has nothing to do with trust and you know it, Adalia Montclair."

Oh shit, he'd double named her. She'd really screwed up then, but she didn't see it. "What are you talking about, Dad?"

"You have no real proof that this billionaire dude did anything wrong."

"Yeah, okay, maybe," she said in rapid succession, and he rose and came around to her side of the table, then took the seat beside her.

"My girl, open your eyes. This man is obviously crazy about you or he wouldn't go to the trouble of trying to make your damn dream come true. You really think he'd do that if he wasn't serious? I hate to break it to you, but men don't do anything for women unless they're crazy about them."

"I don't know." She blinked and bit her bottom lip. "I don't know if I trust him."

"Bullshit," he replied, and she started. Her father hardly ever swore. "You're not worried about whether you can trust him or not. You're being stubborn about this because you don't want to admit defeat."

"That's not true," she grumbled, but it was.

"You're definitely your mother's child. She was a stubborn woman if ever there was one. Beautiful as the sun, just like you, but so stubborn she could've given a mule a run for its damn money."

Adalia sighed. "I know, but I'm not like that, I'm just the kind of person who doesn't take handouts. You're the one who taught me that."

"Oh no you don't," he said with a chuckle, "don't you blame this on me. I taught you to seek independence, not to deny any and all help. You're too prideful. You need to learn to let go before there's nothing to let go of and you end up alone."

"I don't know what to say."

"That's okay. It's not me you have to talk to, my girl," he said, patting her on the arm.

"What do I do, Dad?"

"I think you know what you have to do."

Adalia rose from the chair and gulped. This wouldn't be easy, but her father was right. She'd been too stubborn, she should've heard him out, but it was so much easier to assume the worst, to believe that he'd never wanted her in the first place.

At least, not as a lover.

He pulled her into a bear hug then stroked her hair for comfort. "You'd better hurry. Opportunities like this one don't come around too often, you can believe that." He pushed her away with a grin.

Adalia hurried for the door then paused to check her reflection in the mirror above the entrance hall table. She looked good. Sad, but good.

"Thanks, Dad," she called back over her shoulder.

"Hurry up."

She rushed out the door and down the stairs, heart pounding against her rib cage, trying to smash right out and flop onto the concrete. It was on the line now, her heart, future, body, and soul.

This was it.

Chapter Twenty-Three

The drive over chewed through Adalia's nerves like her old customer on an éclair. What would he say?

She nibbled on her bottom lip hard and tasted blood, then swore and licked her lips to staunch the tiny trickle. She wasn't in her right mind. What if he saw her and slammed the door in her face because of how she'd treated him?

Adalia turned into the driveway and continued a stream of curses right up until she parked outside his front door. She couldn't help it. This terrified her. Rejection and failure were her two main fears and they floated above her head like a haze.

"Come on, you can do this, you can talk to him. He won't reject you, otherwise why would he have called you like twenty times the other day?" She chanted the words over again, so they'd sink into her soul and chase away the fear.

It didn't really work though.

She stared up at the white face of his mansion with its empty windows, staring out on the city. It was far enough away from the central area to be safe, and close enough to be within reach. Perfectly situated for a man of Trent's stature, of course.

Riiiiiing.

What now? She switched off the car and reached into her bag, fumbling for her smartphone in its depths. Maybe it was him, calling to ask how she was, or maybe to offer her the bakery again.

She'd love to hear his voice. But the caller ID was hidden.

She swept her thumb across the green phone icon. "Hello?"

"Hey, I had to call and find out if you was okay." DeShawn's voice rang out, and that frustration at him grew again. He was always in the way, interfering and causing trouble when she didn't need him.

"What do you want, DeShawn? I'm kinda in the middle of something here."

"We need to talk." She'd heard that from him millions of times in the past months, and she was so over it.

"No, we don't."

"Why?"

"Because I say so. We don't need to talk about anything. It's over between us and I don't want you in my life anymore. I've told you that at least twenty bajillion times but you just don't get the point. It's over between us, DeShawn. I want nothing to do with you."

He went quiet for a minute then sniffed. "Told ya, I won't take no for no answer."

She rolled her eyes. "We have that in common then, double negatives aside."

"Huh?"

"Nothing. Don't call this number again." She hung up and tucked the phone back into her bag.

Riiiiiing.

She didn't bother picking it up or checking the caller ID – it would be him calling back. He didn't know when no meant no, and he'd had that problem when they'd dated, too. She'd fallen for him out of desperation, and because he'd looked at her as if he wanted her.

At the time she'd felt fat and disgusted with herself. She'd needed the muscly wannabe gangsta for the self-esteem boost, but those days were gone.

Adalia was big and beautiful. She'd accepted that long ago. She didn't need a man to confirm her beauty, not a pot-smoking ghetto broke dude or a go-getter billionaire with an alpha-male complex.

But she did need him in other ways. In every other way.

Riiiiiiing.

That ringtone would have to change, it annoyed her to the core now. She brought out the phone again, ignored the missed calls, and put it on silent so she wouldn't be caught out while she 'stalked' Trent in his own home.

That was kinda creepy. She laughed at herself, then paused and sighed.

Adalia grimaced and squished the steering wheel. She could still drive away. What if he wasn't even home? The gates were open, but that didn't mean he was inside the massive mansion. Maybe he left them like that out of habit, because his alarm system was that good.

Billionaires were crazy like that.

Adalia swiveled and looked at the garage. His car was parked in front and so was… whose Porsche was that? She'd seen it somewhere before, but she couldn't quite place it.

Likely that Withnail Harrington guy. God, she'd scared him the last time, she owed him an apology for her behavior regardless of what had gone on between her and Trent.

Adalia got out of the car and closed the door as quietly as she could. She wanted the element of surprise on her side, to catch him off guard and stop him from kicking her out before she'd said her piece.

She crept up to the front door and made to ring the bell, but it was ajar. That was weird – it made things easier though. She pressed it open and listened for him, turning her head left and right.

He was probably in the living room having a drink with Mr. Harrington. She hurried in that direction and the muffled sound of talking confirmed her suspicions. She paused and frowned. That didn't sound like a man, though.

Adalia stalked up to the living room door and pressed her ear to it.

"I think she just wanted your money and that was it. She didn't care about you as a person, Trent, baby. You see that, right?"

"Had enough," Trent said, and Adalia gripped the door handle to open up.

"Adalia Montclair," the woman said, and she stopped midway. That voice was…

The vision of the Porsche and the timbre of the woman's tone crashed together in her mind. Michelle Van Heerden was in the living room with her man. Michelle.

The molten lava was back, and she got down on both knees and glared through the keyhole. At least the bitch had her clothes on.

"You should have told her you weren't ready for anything because you were waiting for me." Michelle wore a slinky pink number, and stood in front of Trent, who was on one of the chairs, leaning back and staring off into space.

His expression was emotionless, painted with the numbness Adalia had lived with the past few weeks.

Her heart went out to him, and she stood to open the door again. But Michelle Van Heerden wasn't done yet, and her sentiment rang through the wood of the door, driving up the heat past molten, to sheer surface-of-the-sun temperatures.

"I know it's tough for you, babe, but there's no use longing for someone who doesn't want you. It's clear that she was a user and abuser."

Adalia was gratified for a moment; apparently, he'd been longing for her after all.

Adalia heard the sound of a zipper, and material hitting the floor. She pressed her eye to the keyhole again. Michelle was naked, but for a thong and bra. She was flawless in that, so skinny and toned.

If Trent touched her, Adalia would lose it. She couldn't stand this a second longer.

He was still mute and staring dead ahead, blinking occasionally, but he hadn't asked the bitch to leave him alone. Why not?

"I've waited so long to be with you, to touch you and hold you. To ride that fat cock of yours. God, this is going to be exquisite. I'll make you forget all about that slut."

"Adalia," he whispered, shaking his head.

Michelle nodded. "Yes, that one. You'll forget all about her after I've done you right." She climbed onto his lap, straddling him, and gyrated backward and forward, then moved her hips in circles. "Don't you want a taste?"

Trent didn't answer, and Adalia couldn't make out his expression. This was too much – why didn't he push her away? If he really didn't want her, if they weren't an item, why didn't he push that horrible woman away?

"Yeah, now you're mine, look into my eyes," Michelle whispered, then lowered her head and kissed him. Slurping noises filled the room, and there was an audible snap in Adalia's brain. DONE!

Adalia kicked the door open. "What the fuck is going on here?"

She charged into the room and the pair sprang apart. Trent swayed slightly then focused on her and his eyes widened.

"Adalia?"

Michelle Van Heerden stood, wearing nothing but a thong and lacy bra and she didn't attempt to cover herself up.

"Ms. Montclair, what a pleasant surprise."

-To be continued in Book 2-

If you liked the story, please take a moment to leave a review.

Here is a preview of the **next book** you may also enjoy:

Love Forgiven: Tenacious Billionaire BWWM Romance Series, Book 2

"**THEY WANT** them Black Forest cheesecakes done in thirty," Melanie said, chewing on a stick of gum.

Adalia sighed and blinked a couple times. "I'm not a miracle worker. Besides, I hardly think anyone in the store is going to riot if I don't get it out on time."

Annie's Market specialized in nothing but providing loads of baked goods to as many customers as possible – in short, the quality was terrible. The recipes in the bakery section were set and Adalia's creativity was stifled, but a job was a job and God knew she needed the money after that debauchery with Trent.

Melanie shuffled out of the kitchen and the doors swung in her wake. The girl had about as much finesse as a bull on steroids. She'd worked there for a week as Adalia's manager, and it was difficult to respect her.

Failure, failure, failure. The word repeated itself in her head.

Measure out the flour, *failure*, weigh the sugar, *failure*, beat the eggs, *failure*. It didn't matter what she did or which way she looked at things. She'd messed up. Big time.

Melanie shoved back into the kitchen. "Store manager says to get 'em done or you're in trouble."

"You went to the store manager?" Adalia stared at her and shook her head.

"Yeah, and there's some guy here to see you."

Adalia's heart leapt into her throat, and she stopped moving completely. Screw the Black Forest cakes, what if Trent had arrived? Mortification paralyzed her; she was glued to the spot.

The last thing she'd want was the billionaire to see her slumming it in a tiny store bakery.

"Who?" Adalia whispered.

Melanie raised an eyebrow. "Derick or something, I didn't hear proper. Get them cakes ready." She turned and charged out again, still chewing gum like it was her air to breathe.

"Derick," Adalia said to herself, shaking her head in confusion. Who the hell was Derick? She dusted off her hands on her grubby apron and strolled out of the kitchen and into the kiosk area.

It wasn't Derick; it was DeShawn.

"Hey baby," he murmured, resting his elbows on top of the glass case, and gazing into her eyes. "I've been thinking about you all day."

"I'm honored," she replied, and the sarcasm was lost on him. She didn't want to see Trent, but she surely didn't want to see her ex-boyfriend either. He'd pretty much messed with her mind for long enough, and she didn't need that added pressure or drama.

"You working here now?"

"No," she grumbled. "I just come here to work out."

"Huh?"

"Nothing," she said with a sweet smile. "What do you want, DeShawn? I've got things to do right now." She glanced out over the empty store and made eye contact with the manager.

He glared at her and tilted his head to the side like the oversized buzzard he was. "Hurry up," he mouthed then tapped his cheap Kmart watch.

She forced herself not to roll her eyes at the authority figure. Once upon a time, she'd loved baking, but that was when she'd been able to create something from fresh, not stick to the plan, no matter how disgusting it was.

"Baby?" DeShawn's voice interrupted her train of thought.

"What is it?" She snapped her focus back to his face. "Like I said, I'm busy."

"And I said I want you back."

Agony erupted in her chest, pushing aside every other emotion. She'd been through so much, tasted a hint of success and then fallen hard. All she wanted was to get back on her feet and move on with her life, but DeShawn was back.

"Why? Give me one good reason why."

"Because I love you, baby," he said, leaning over the case of day-old cakes to grab at her arm. She didn't jerk it away and he managed to bring it up and take hold of her hand instead. He brought the tips of her fingers to his lips and kissed them gently.

There wasn't heat like there was with Trent, but it still brought out something in her. Something good. A long forgotten memory of what it was like to be touched by a person who cared.

Did DeShawn truly care?

"I don't trust you, and I don't need that," she said, pulling her hand from his grasp and wiping the back on her apron with a sour expression.

"You never gave me a chance to prove myself to you. I love you so much, baby, and you ain't never given me the chance to show it."

"What are you talking about?" she spat, trembling from head to toe. "I gave you every chance in the world to show your love for me and you didn't make any effort whatsoever."

"I came to your daddy's place to talk to you."

"What?!" Adalia laughed out loud and the manager shot her a look of pure loathing. "I'm not talking about after I dumped your sorry ass. By then, it was too late. I'm talking about before. Because when it really mattered, you didn't give a crap."

"I was high a lot of the time."

"Precisely." Adalia gripped the low-slung counter with both hands.

Melanie appeared beside her. "You gotta get back to work. The Black Forest cakes aren't gonna bake themselves."

"What the hell does a store need two managers for?" Adalia blurted, then snapped her mouth shut.

Melanie glared at her for a minute then charged off again, muttering to herself.

That meant more trouble for her. The bakery manager chewed and steamed her way over to the store manager and flung her arms around, describing what Adalia had said in minute detail, apparently.

"You realize how busy I am, right?" Adalia breathed slowly, through the anger and disappointment in herself.

"Yeah, true that. Look, girl, I can't live without you. I'm not gonna treat you bad again. Only give you what you deserve. You gotta believe me."

"No, DeShawn, all I 'gotta' do is work and keep this damn job so I can earn enough money to make rent this damn month."

"So, come live wit' me." DeShawn grinned and spread his arms wide, then scratched beneath the line of his do-rag. His muscles rippled beneath his tank top, but she didn't have that spark with him.

Maybe she'd never feel that chemistry again. Hell, she'd probably imagined it in the first place.

"I'm not moving in with you, DeShawn. There's no question about that in my mind."

"Aight," he said, then rapped his knuckles on the glass counter. "So lemme take you on a date."

The store manager held up a hand to Melanie's face, then walked past her and marched in Adalia's direction.

Some of the shelves in the store leaned skew, the cans had a layer of dust which matched the grime on the front windows. Hardly any sunlight made it through to the back, so the fluorescents buzzing and clicking overhead made perfect sense.

"You need to leave now," Adalia murmured, bracing herself for the complaints from the manager. "I ain't leaving," DeShawn said. The manager, Mr. Hubbard, was almost at the kiosk.

"What?"

"I ain't leaving until you say you'll go on a date with me."

"Do you realize I could lose my job over this? Do you even care?"

"I care about you, but I ain't gonna take no for no answer, and you need to see that, girl." DeShawn seemed oblivious to the risk he'd put her under just by showing up. She was at the end of her tether with him and with everything else.

Mr. Hubbard was steps away.

"Fine, I'll go on a date with you. Just get outta here!" She hissed it at him, then plastered up a broad smile.

"Adalia," Hubbard said, stopping beside DeShawn. "I'd like to see you in the kitchen for a moment."

"Yes, sir," she said, still with that sick, fake smile on her lips. It suited how she felt inside: nauseated by the situation and what she had to do each day. She was a sellout.

"On Friday, baby," DeShawn called out after.

The kitchen doors swung shut behind her.

If you enjoyed this sample then look for **Love Forgiven: Tenacious Billionaire BWWM Romance Series, Book 2**.

Here is a preview of **another story** you may enjoy:

Love Restrained - Fervent Billionaire BWWM Romance Series, Book 1

"**EXHALE SLOWLY**," the yoga instructor said in a soothing voice. Alexandra exhaled her breath and relaxed her muscles. As she exhaled, she consciously focused on releasing all of her worries. Her body was in the bridge pose, so her navel faced the twirling ceiling fan.

"Inhale through your nose," came the second instruction. Alexandra inhaled and the sound of her breath filled her ears. She held the pose for what seemed like a lifetime as the base of her neck pressed against the floor.

"Release," came the blessed instruction, finally. Automatically, Alexandra moved into corpse pose. She had been practicing yoga for three months and was finally feeling confident about her poses. She knew that there was still a long way to go, but she was getting there. Her mind was relaxed as she felt the warm caress of the sunlight travel along her torso. A smile spread across her face as she focused on existing entirely in the moment. Without thought, she moved fluidly between all of the yoga positions.

Her eyes opened and her mind returned when the instructor ended the session, "Thank you for attending, *Namaste*."

"*Namaste*," Alexandra replied with her palms together. As she rolled up her mat, she looked around at the other patrons. All were covered in sweat, all wearing modern yoga shorts and tops. Only the instructor wore the loose-fitting, traditional clothes of *Kundalini* yoga. Karen, the instructor, stood at the head of the class in conversation with a few of the patrons.

Turning away from everyone else, Alexandra studied her figure in the large mirror that lined the wall of the room. Her eyes wandered across her own body and she felt pleasure at seeing the results of her many yoga sessions. The pink and black yoga pants fit perfectly along her dark calves and hips. Slender, yet toned, she admired her own hourglass figure in the mirror. Her eyes glanced at her glistening ebony skin and the few beads of sweat that dotted her skin from the overly warm room. She released her curly hair from the clasp of a bun and watched as it cascaded down her shoulders.

With a broad smile, she turned to leave the room. She walked toward the door and placed her hand on the warm metal doorknob. As the door pushed forward, she looked over her shoulder to say goodbye to her instructor. She noticed Karen and a man speaking with each other, their eyes looking at Alexa's toned figure. Dismissing the glances, she turned away with a cheery wave.

A few blocks down the street was her favorite café, the one that she went to after yoga class. As she walked there, she could feel the eyes of other people watching her—mostly men. Not long ago after making a steady income, she had moved to a more upscale segment of town. As one of the few African-Americans in town, she drew stares that ranged from curious to desirous whenever she went out. She did not mind the ogling, but it was the catcalls that ate at her. Catcalls were so vulgar and seemed cowardly. If someone wanted to speak to her, then she would prefer that they were up front with her. She felt that a real man would be one who says what he means and does not just yell something out of a speeding car window.

If you enjoyed this sample then look for **Love Restrained - Fervent Billionaire BWWM Romance Series, Book 1**.

Here is a preview of **another story** you may enjoy:

Love Eluded: Audacious Billionaire BWWM Romance Series, Book 1

CHANTE GREEN knew she was going to be late for work…again.

"Shit…," she mumbled, impatiently tapping her foot as she craned her neck to see if the bus was anywhere in sight.

She could almost see the look of annoyance on the face of her supervisor, Nurse Betty Lebowitz. It was the third time this month alone and Chante knew she was hanging by a thread. She could lose her job at New York General Hospital, and she needed that now more than ever.

Chante genuinely hoped that Nurse Betty would be a little sympathetic and cut her some slack. After all, the supervisor was familiar with the reason Chante was under a tremendous amount of pressure. Her brother Markey had ALS or Amyotrophic Lateral Sclerosis, also known as Lou Gehrig's disease.

A catastrophic disease that was initially misdiagnosed, Markey now had only partial control of his legs. Looking back, he was always clumsy as a child, often falling or stumbling, but everyone said it was just a phase and he'll eventually outgrow it. But as the years progressed, Chante noticed the slurred speech. Her mom eventually took him to a specialist who, after rigorous testing declared the boy was in the second stages of ALS.

Things became even more difficult when Chante's dad contracted malaria and eventually died from it. Chante and her mom, both heartbroken over the sudden death, struggled to meet the special needs that were required to deal with ALS. Her mom, having had experience in caring for sick children, took on most of the responsibilities. When swallowing became too hard, they took turns giving him food through a feeding tube. Mom would bathe him; help him use the bathroom; exercise his arms and legs to prevent atrophy, until her son's disease took its toll on her as well.

Driving one night to buy medicine at a nearby pharmacy, she was too preoccupied to notice the red light at a street intersection and was hit on the driver's side by a passing truck. She was in a coma for three days before she succumbed to her injuries. At nineteen years old, Chante was left with an enormous responsibility towards a brother who was not even of her own blood, but who meant more to her than anything in the whole world. He was her only family.

Chante didn't remember much of her early childhood years, except shuttling from one foster home to another. At six years old, she was considered too old by most couples wanting to adopt a baby. The shy and gawky black girl with soulful green eyes was never chosen. Unable to find a good family for her, city officials decided to turn her over to the State Institution for Unwanted Children. On the eve of her departure, a woman came in, noticed her cringing in a corner, and approached her.

Chante believed she was an angel with blond hair falling softly around her shoulder. But it was the sweet voice that calmed her enough to reach for the hand that was offered to her. The woman was enamored with the emaciated child and decided to adopt her. The lady, Hannah Green, brought her home and introduced her to her husband, Caleb, a Mulatto who was delighted to see her. Chante felt an instant kinship with the dark-skinned stranger. Hannah made her feel like the daughter they never had. Both were missionaries who went to far-flung places on medical missions.

Chante spent her growing years travelling to places most children would have found depressing. No electricity, no running water, and sometimes just a hut to sleep on at night, if they were lucky. Otherwise, it had to be in a tent or under the stars. Children with malaria, TB, pneumonia, measles, and countless other maladies constantly filled their days.

From her adoptive parents, Chante learned
compassion, dedication, and sympathy for the sick. No
one was turned away. There was always room for one
more.

Chante blossomed under their care. The lost look in
her eyes gradually changed to confidence. She learned
her ABC's under Acacia trees with other children.
Instead of children's books, medical books were her
constant companion. She couldn't read most of the
words, but the pictures amazed her. It was no surprise
that she declared she would become a doctor someday.
She changed her mind after she found her passion
working alongside the nurses, who took care of their
patients day-in and day-out.

It was during one of these missions that her mom
and dad discovered that they were expecting a baby.
Chante's innate insecurity returned. She knew she was
adopted and was afraid to be given away again. Her
parents, seeing the troubled look on her face, assured
her that she would always be a part of their family.
They loved her so much like she was their very own,
they said. That restored her confidence so much so that
when the baby finally arrived, Chante immediately fell
in love with the little bundle of crinkly skin and puffy
eyes. No one seeing them for the first time would ever
doubt they were brother and sister. They looked so

much alike… same curly hair and bronzed chocolaty skin complexion.

When Chante's dad contracted malaria and eventually died from it, they moved to a smaller house. Maintaining the big sprawling colonial house where Chante grew up became too much for her mom. Money was scarce with the little pension she was receiving from her work as a missionary and Chante was in her last year in high school.

If you enjoyed this sample then look for **Love Eluded: Audacious Billionaire BWWM Romance Series, Book 1**.

Other books by Shyla Starr:

Elusive Billionaire Romance Series

Lonely Billionaire Romance Series

Ardent Billionaire Romance Series

Fervent Billionaire BWWM Romance Series

Audacious Billionaire BWWM Romance Series

Get the latest update on new releases from the author at:

http://shylastarr.com/newsletter

About the Author - Shyla Starr

Shyla currently specializes in writing interracial romance stories and is a huge fan of the alpha male. Simply put, there just aren't enough stories about mixed couple romances, which is something she is aiming to fix.

Being a bookworm all her life, when Shyla discovered men she also realized how easy it was to fulfill her fantasies through her writing.

When not writing and fantasizing about men, Shyla enjoys dancing, reading and chilling with her friends.